Eva Hanagan was born and brought up in the Highlands of Scotland. She became a member of the Foreign Office staff in 1945 and was posted to Vienna for four years. She married an army officer and life as a Service wife took her to Germany and the Middle East. They have two sons, and since her husband John's retirement from the Army they have lived in Sussex.

ALICE

~

Eva Hanagan

WARNER BOOKS

A *Warner* Book

First published in Great Britain
by Warner Books in 1997

Copyright © Eva Hanagan 1997

The moral right of the author has been asserted.

Typeset in Ehrhardt by M Rules
Printed and bound in Great Britain by
Clays Ltd, St Ives plc

Warner Books
A Division of
Little, Brown and Company (UK)
Brettenham House
Lancaster Place
London WC2E 7EN

To Judy and Gil Prewett

1

~

It was with reluctance that Alice opened the door that connected her large and comfortable bedroom with its adjoining dressing room. Entering that room distressed her but she was aware of the necessity of opening its window from time to time.

The room was ill-proportioned, being too narrow for its height, and on its air there hung still a faint suggestion of attar of roses and a trace of surgical spirit. But there was also something less tangible which even the sunlight of early summer dappling the carpet could not dispel – an undertone of bleak despair.

The worn carpet had had one edge of its patterned border shorn off in order that it should fit the room and the severed remnant had then been cut and neatly bound to provide two rugs, one of which lay beside the narrow bed, the second in front of the cracked washbasin. The tiny grate of the Victorian fireplace was empty, its starkness undisguised by as much as a handful of pine cones or a bowl of immortelles. The furnishings were sparse, and every item – rickety basket chair, spindly legged table, narrow chest covered with faded chintz and masquerading as a window-seat, clumsy wardrobe – conveyed the same impression of gloomy parsimony which contrasted so strangely with the comfort that prevailed in the rest of Fernhurst.

That her Aunt Sophie should have elected to spend her last years in such uncongenial surroundings was unthinkable. But Alice could not prevent herself thinking about it, although no reasonable answer ever resulted.

The last time she had seen her Aunt, a few years before her death, Alice had come down from London to attend her grandmother's funeral. Sophie had then prepared her own bedroom for Alice, fearing that the other rooms, so long unoccupied, might be uncomfortably damp. She had explained that for the last few months she had taken to sleeping in the little dressing room in order to be close at hand to tend her mother. One could now only conjecture that Sophie had become so accustomed to the room as to have ceased to be aware of its discomfort and ugliness or, even if aware, had felt too dispirited and tired to attend to her own well-being with the result that a make-shift arrangement had eventually acquired permanence. Poor dear Sophie.

It occurred to Alice that only since she had come to live in Fernhurst had she begun to think of her aunt as 'poor' Sophie. But, she admitted to herself, the sad truth is that I never really thought much about her at all, certainly not as much as I ought to have done. I made the occasional visit, although, in all honesty, the emphasis lay on 'occasional'. She had made no visits at all after her grandmother's death, but there had been Oliver's ill-heath and time had slipped away so quickly . . . Still, I was punctilious about sending birthday and Christmas cards and lovingly selected gifts and I did write her a nice newsy letter from time to time. She recalled that she had not neglected to make regular telephone calls although in the last years of Sophie's life it had not been possible to talk directly to her, the telephone being downstairs in the hall and Sophie having been confined to her bed, here in this horrid room.

There had always been Nancy. Nancy to assure her that Sophie was comfortable, Nancy to relay her good wishes and love to Sophie and her promises to come down some day to see her. Nancy to tell her that there was nothing which she could usefully do for her aunt; and surely that really had been the case, Alice told herself, trying to shake free the sense of guilt and not wholly succeeding, the sin of omission being one of the most elusive from which to escape by self-absolution. In any case, she reminded herself in self-justification, I had visualised Aunt Sophie ensconced once more in her nice sunny room on the other side of the landing; in bed, yes, but sitting up busy with some needle-work, drinking tea with visiting friends, or perhaps just lying comfortably with her eyes closed listening to music on the radio and enjoying her well-earned rest. I had never imagined her lying here almost completely immobilised by that cruel stroke. 'Not able to get about much' was how Nancy, concerned no doubt to save Alice from distress, had put it.

A dead tortoiseshell butterfly lay on the window-ledge, dry and brittle as an autumn leaf and still entangled in the deceptively fragile web into which it had blundered on one now distant day. Alice pinched it between finger and thumb and cast it outside where it was soon lost to sight among the blossoms of the rose that clothed the wall below the window. Alice leaned out, breathing the warm scented air, resting her eyes on the soft billows of the Downs that rose beyond and behind Fernhurst. Light scudding clouds chequered the grass with fleeting shadows, and the grazing sheep looked like flecks of spume on a gently heaving sea.

With her back to the room, its disturbing implications out of sight, Alice tried to recapture the atmosphere of

Fernhurst as she remembered it. Fernhurst had been a house of women: her grandmother, Aunt Sophie, her own mother, the friends who came to call, Cook and Nancy in attendance somewhere in the background and all forever remembered in this peaceful and enduring setting. There had been Grandfather too but as he had died when she was barely seven he was recalled with less ease. They probably spoiled me, but in the nicest possible way, thought Alice. Raised voices or discord of any kind never featured in these memories. At the slightest sign of impending altercation or disagreement, Grandmother would quietly insist that she would not tolerate 'any unpleasantness'. In deference to her authority, which was of the iron order imposed to such good effect by the apparently delicate and gentle, Grandmother had invariably enjoyed the privilege of the last word.

It was understandable, thought Alice, sharply closing the window, that as a child I took Sophie, gentle self-effacing Sophie, for granted but what I cannot forgive myself for is that I then relegated her to the well-thumbed pages of memory and selfishly ignored her continuing existence as a person in her own right.

But if, in fact, Sophie herself had considered that Alice had neglected her, then she must surely have forgiven her as she had left her everything that she had had to leave. 'The little of which I die possessed' was the curious and modest wording in which Sophie had expressed her intention that Alice should inherit Fernhurst, its contents and a healthy portfolio of investments.

Here in Fernhurst there was no escaping the tangible reminders of Sophie – or, at least, the evidence of how she had occupied her leisure time. Scattered throughout the house were numerous cushions whose covers Sophie had painstakingly worked in gros point; the drawers of the sideboard were crammed with exquisitely embroidered table-linen; crocheted bedspreads mantled every bed in the house like frosted snow. Had Sophie herself finally tired of these reminders of what had occupied the years of her life – could that be the reason why this room alone contained not one shred of her handwork?

All of Nancy's long working years had been spent in Fernhurst, but beyond the well-cared-for state of the house nothing remained to remind Alice of her presence. Well, not quite nothing; there was one overlooked personal belonging. In the kitchen Nancy had always hung a daily calendar with a thick little pad of detachable pages, one for every day. Below the date each page bore a quotation no doubt chosen to furnish the reader with a message of spiritual edification or mental stimulation to carry one through the day's vicissitudes. Nancy's calendar for the previous year of 1984 remained hanging over the kitchen sink. The topmost page, Alice had been slightly startled to observe, bore the date of Sophie's death and, although Nancy had remained in the house until after the funeral, she had not torn off that page. It was as though time had stopped. Perhaps for Nancy, in a sense, it had. The quote for that day came from *Paradise Lost*:

> Freely we serve
> Because we freely love, as in our will
> To love or not; in this we stand or fall.

I still haven't done anything about Nancy, Alice guiltily reflected. The days seem to pass so quickly. But that is no excuse; it's just a matter of getting down to it. One had to acknowledge that the older one grew the faster time seemed to race. How did it come about that she was approaching sixty, well, to be exact, fifty-nine, within what seemed such a short space of time? Alice continued to gaze out of the window at a countryside which appeared unchanged.

The telephone was ringing, its repetitive clamour rising from the hall and tearing through the hushed stillness of the house. Alice ran to answer it, glad of the distraction, pleased by the nimbleness with which she sped down the stairs, token of an agility which distanced her from the final plight of her aunt.

'There you are at last! I was beginning to think you'd gone out.'

Alice held the receiver a little distance from her ear; the voice at the other end was loud as well as admonitory.

'Sorry, I was just . . .' Alice stopped herself. Why should she explain? What was it about Miss Vine that always put one on the defensive, obliged one to make excuses?

But Cornelia Vine was ignoring her half-finished reply, her voice continuing as though anything that Alice might have to say was of no consequence unless it was in reply to a direct question, and even then she might well choose to ignore it.

'Got your man there?'

Alice stifled her annoyance at the accuracy of Miss Vine's bland assumption that 'your man' could now refer only to the aged Fred who tended her garden.

'No. He only comes on Fridays. His rheumatism is getting worse, you see.' Damn! There I go again, explaining.

'Botheration! I wanted you to send him round here to start the mower for me. Can't get it to budge. He shouldn't pander to his rheumatism, always a great mistake to give in to minor ailments – I'd tell him that, if I were you.'

'Have you tried Tom?'

'No good. Haven't you heard? He's dancing attendance on that Cornford woman these days. Spends all his time at Upper Lea, cleaning out her fishpond, if you please. Thinks he's on to a good thing there.'

'Oh now, surely that's a little unfair. Tom's always so . . .'

'Could you just pop over yourself and give the starter a yank or two? Wouldn't take you a minute. Grass'll be up to my hocks if I can't get it cut soon.'

'Well, I'm not sure, actually I . . .'

'Good. I knew you wouldn't let me down. See you soon then.'

There was a disagreeable rattle in Alice's ear as Miss Vine fumbled her receiver back on to its rest. Miss Vine's telephone, as Alice had observed, was so nearly submerged in a clutter of books and papers that the wonder was that its owner could locate it at all, but she demonstrably did and with a frequency which Alice was not alone in finding inconvenient.

Why do we all run at her beck and call? she wondered crossly, searching for her car keys in the hall-table drawer.

I suppose, Alice thought, as she negotiated the turns and twists of the narrow country lane with less care than they warranted, I suppose the hold she has over us – Barbara, Clare, Thelma, Mary, herself, all 'my old girls' according to Miss Vine's proprietorial phraseology – is that we feel strangely flattered by being treated as children, and Miss Vine is probably the only person left who can see us in that light. Not that any of them would admit to that, preferring to ascribe their craven willingness to indulge Miss Vine's every whim to natural affection towards their old head-mistress or, at the very least, a decent sense of duty and loyalty. In Alice's own case there was the matter of her feeling of guilt which Miss Vine doubtless sensed and was not reluctant to exploit. Cornelia had been a life-long friend of Sophie. In the end she became the only surviving friend of her youth. Alice suspected that in Miss Vine's opinion she had shamefully failed in her duty towards her aunt.

Nothing to that effect had actually been said, but Miss Vine, while rarely reluctant to frankly express her opinion, was also an accomplished mistress of the art of conveying criticism without resort to outright statement.

Miss Vine was in her little front garden busy ridding her rose bushes of greenfly by the simple expedient of running her fingers over their infested stems. In lofty disregard for the warmth of the June day, she wore a grey tweed skirt of comfortable dimensions and, hanging over it, a linen-buttoned cream blouse which looked as though it might once have been the upper-half of a winceyette nightdress, which was indeed the case.

'Goodness!' she exclaimed, wiping her green-stained fingers on the seat of her skirt. 'Fancy taking the car! I'd have thought you could walk on a lovely day like this.'

'The car saves time,' said Alice, hoping to imply that Miss Vine's summons had thoughtlessly interrupted some busy activity.

'My dear that was thoughtful of you, but I wouldn't have minded being kept waiting a little. Still, it's nice to know that you appreciate that the older one grows the less patient one becomes. Time flies so – I sometimes wonder where the hours go!' She was peering at a deep crack in the lichened gatepost as though suspecting that some of the missing hours had escaped into its damp depths.

'Just look at that! I swear it's getting wider by the day. It's months since the wretched Tom promised to put in a new post. I'm very disappointed in that man, he's proved himself so unreliable. Not like my girls. They never let me down!' Slipping her arm round Alice's waist, Miss Vine rewarded her with a surprisingly youthful grin which gave an airing to strong square teeth whose colour time had mellowed to the tint of ripe melon seed.

'Come,' she said, propelling Alice firmly down the garden

path (a manoeuvre well suited to Miss Vine's skills), 'I'll introduce you to the monster.'

The old mower that stood on the back lawn had a ponderous undefeated air about it as though it dared anyone to budge it by so much as an inch; judging by the length of the grass around it, it had been some time since anyone had been foolhardy enough to take up the challenge.

'Do you know,' said Miss Vine, aiming a vicious little kick at its smug fat tyres, 'I sometimes think that if only I could start the mower I could be completely independent!'

Some quarter of an hour later, although to Alice it seemed longer, the machine, responding to the last of a series of frenzied yanks on the starter cord, spluttered into indignant growling life.

Her hair plastered to her neck with sweat, and convinced that her arm was within a fraction of being dislocated, Alice looked around in astonished triumph for Miss Vine. She looked in vain. A minute before she had been all too obtrusively there, exhorting, criticising, proffering a rag to dry the plugs, suggesting the use of a hot-water bottle to warm up the carburettor, but now, at the moment of success, with Alice ready to hand the vibrating monster into her hands, Miss Vine was nowhere in sight.

Afraid that if she left it unattended for even a second the engine would die on her – it was already coughing in a peevish aggrieved fashion – Alice resigned herself to putting the machine into gear and getting on with the job. Up and down the generous length of the lawn she toiled, stumbling over the exposed roots of the cankered apple trees and heaving the machine round their boles.

From time to time as she jerked her head upwards to toss her straying hair from her eyes, Alice could glimpse Miss Vine's pretty cottage drowsing in the sunshine, its cool interior beckoning invitingly from inside its open back door. Tiny wisps of cloud floated almost motionlessly in a deep blue sky and a thrush sang from the top of a lilac bush – at least Alice supposed it was singing; its beak was parted but the noise of the mower drowned any such feeble competition. The herbaceous border seemed to shimmer in the heat, but Alice realised that that could be an illusion occasioned by the shaking of her eyeballs.

Not until the mower had been brought to a juddering halt over the very piece of yellowed grass from which it had been cajoled into motion did Miss Vine reappear, emerging insouciantly from the open door and bearing a tea tray.

'Well done, my dear,' she called out into the blessed quiet, her voice still as resonant as Alice remembered it when it had soared over bowed heads at morning assembly all of fifty years ago. 'Grub's up!' This in a jolly, rallying tone, Alice having not yet responded: legs trembling, she was still clutching the handle of the mower, uncertain if she dared attempt to stand unsupported.

Miss Vine placed the tray on the heavy round iron table that stood in the shade of an apple tree and sat herself down on the bench beside it. 'Oh dear!' She was looking quizzically at the grass still sprouting lushly under the table, a dark green oasis in the shorn yellowed expanse where Alice had laboured. 'You must have forgotten to move the table, Alice. Never mind, it'll all need another going-over with the blades set a little lower and this patch can be cut then. No!' She raised a hand in disavowal. 'Don't think I'm criticising, dear, you were quite right to set them high for the first cut. The grass had got rather out of hand!'

'But I don't think I'll have time . . .'

'Not before we've had our tea, of course! Goodness, I didn't mean that you should do it right away, dear. There's no immediate rush. Now do come and sit down, Alice, it's

not wise to stand in the full sun for too long, you look far
too flushed.' Miss Vine patted the bench beside her. 'Come
along now!'

Alice sat down thankfully and rubbed her damp grass-
stained hands furtively on her handkerchief. It would not
have surprised her if Miss Vine sent her off to wash them.
Still, she thought, glancing sideways at the two rock buns on
the tray, it didn't really matter; it was not as though she felt
tempted to eat anything.

'Tell me, Alice, how is it all going? Do you feel really settled in by now?' She enunciated 'settled in' as though it were
enclosed in inverted commas. The description, and its vari-
ation of 'settled down' had been much employed by Miss
Vine in her end of term reports. It conjured up for Alice a
picture of a hen resignedly arranging herself on a nest.

'Yes. Well, more or less.'

'It must be quite a large house to manage unaided. In
your grandparents' day there was always staff – the war
brought that sort of thing to an end, of course. You haven't
any help at all, have you? No? But then a woman on her
own doesn't create work in a house. Get it straight and it
stays that way.'

Alice tried not to think about the untidy chaos inside
Miss Vine's cottage which looked so deceptively neat from
the outside. But then perhaps Miss Vine wouldn't claim to
have got it straight yet although one might think that four,
or was it five, years of retirement should provide adequate
time in which to accomplish some sort of order, even allowing for her age. Enjoying the advantage of being both owner
and Headmistress of Beech Park, Miss Vine had been in no
hurry to relinquish her life's work and had been in her late
seventies before she had retired – and even then with reluctance. In the later years of her reign her well-honed skills in
the art of delegation had served her well.

'Yes. Yes, I do agree,' Alice said, Miss Vine seeming to expect some response.

'Fernhurst has always been so full of *things*. Your grandfather was such a collector and so catholic in his tastes – this, that and the other, whatever took his fancy. But it did create such a lot of dusting; dear Sophie used to complain about it, I remember.'

'Well it's not too bad now. Nancy cleared a great many pieces away into cupboards. I expect she wanted to cut down on the work when Aunt Sophie needed more attention.'

'Ah yes, the inimitable Nancy! The last of a vanished breed – the old type of faithful servant.'

Alice felt wary. Any moment now and Miss Vine might add, and with justification, 'I don't know what Sophie would have done without Nancy,' and Alice would stand accused. She wondered if Miss Vine knew Nancy's present whereabouts. She might even know the answer to the puzzle which made Alice anxious to trace Nancy and have a talk with her. But to ask for information would be to admit her abysmal ignorance about her aunt's last years.

The thrush that had sung from the lilac bush was now scuffling in the ivy that flourished below the hedge and Miss Vine was crumbling up a rock bun and tossing scorched currants in its direction.

Perhaps it was only awareness of her own shortcomings that made Alice suspect that Miss Vine was deliberately prolonging the conversational pause in the hope that she would be encouraged to ask some questions. But when Miss Vine spoke again, it was to ask Alice if she had yet made up her mind to remain at Fernhurst or whether she might sell the house and return to London.

'I've left my options open – I haven't sold my London house.'

Miss Vine nodded. 'That seems wise. Your son continues

to live there, doesn't he? He manages all right on his own?'

'I expect so!' But David wasn't on his own; there was Sally.

'Well, a personable young man needn't be left alone to his own devices a moment longer than he wishes! They go their own way, the young – with or without our approval. But life is so much less conventional nowadays.'

She knows about Sally, thought Alice, avoiding Miss Vine's eye and pretending an interest in the thrush which had hopped out from the dusty cover of the ivy, resenting perhaps the unsolicited bombardment of carbonised currants. It carried with it a snail which it now banged busily on a paving stone, pausing occasionally to thrust its beak into the widening hole in the shell.

She's been winkling information out of Barbara, Alice thought. Damn. In the past, before her husband's death, Alice had never felt the need to confide in anyone other than Oliver. He had always been there to talk to, always ready to listen, the sole recipient of her anxieties, her hopes, her secrets – no, sharing everything with Oliver had meant no secrets in the real sense of the word. How agreeable life had been without the burden of doubts, worries or knowledge entertained exclusively by oneself! It had been foolish to think that she could ever talk to anyone else again in the knowledge that nothing would be repeated or unwittingly revealed. It would be unfair to blame Barbara; the fault was her own. Her natural caution had atrophied from lack of use.

Something of her distress must have shown in her face. Miss Vine moved a hand towards Alice who promptly clasped her own together in her lap, but whether to conceal their grubbiness or to avoid the intimacy of Miss Vine's sympathetic clasp, Alice was not herself certain.

'It can't be easy for you, dear, you must miss your husband dreadfully. I only met him once, years ago when you were both here on holiday and your David was just a little chap. But Sophie told me what a happy marriage it was. It was perhaps fortunate that she died just before he did – otherwise she would have been so distressed for you, and her suffering was quite enough without that. It would be foolish, if not impertinent, for me to say that you'll get over Oliver's death. Of course you won't. But, given time, I'm quite sure that you'll succeed in coming to terms with it. My dear, you must be wondering how I can possibly know. Of course, in a way, you'd be right. I never did experience the privilege of sharing my whole life with someone whom I deeply loved . . . every day together. But I can imagine it. Try to believe me when I say that you will eventually come to terms with it. People do come to terms with all sorts of sorrows. They have no option.

'Besides, Alice, you were always what I would classify as a resilient child. Oh I know I only had you for a couple of years at Beech Park, but you were between eleven and thirteen at that time and that's a good age to assess a child's potential. That was a difficult period for you, too. You were getting over your father's death then and coping very well as I remember it. I remember so much, you know – well, it's true what they say: that as one grows older the distant past becomes more vivid.'

Alice remembered too. Her mother, her dependable, capable mother suddenly lost, frightened, inaccessible. Her own bewilderment and resentment that her mother was so immersed in her own grief that she had seemed oblivious of Alice's need for comfort and also impervious to her desperate and childish attempts to console her. Their hurried flight home to Fernhurst, to Grandmother and Aunt Sophie, for a visit which had been planned to be short but which had lasted for nearly two years. Dear patient Sophie.

Miss Vine was brisk again. She fired the remains of the bun in the thrush's direction. 'That bird thieves the best of my raspberries and what it and its progeny do to my little cherry crop is nothing short of criminal!' She rose to her feet and, waving away Alice's proffered help, replaced the tea cups on the tray.

'Time you were away, Alice. I can't sit idling all day in the sun, I have things to do!' Alice, thus dismissed, almost believed that it was she who had been taking up Miss Vine's time and not the other way around. She really is quite appalling, Alice thought with a grudging admiration, relieved to find that the sympathy that had been briefly evoked had as rapidly evaporated.

'But before you go, dear, there's something I want you to do for me. Just a minute!' Miss Vine called over her shoulder, already on her way to the house.

She emerged a moment later with three fat books in her hands. 'You can drop these in to Barbara. She can return them to the library for me and I've enclosed a note of the books I want her to take out. I do so hate going into the village in the tripper season. As you've got the car with you it won't take a minute to take them to her.

'The garden's looking rather nice, don't you think?' Miss Vine had paused on the lawn, looking with approval at the freshly mown grass. Glad that she'd forgotten about the necessity for a second cut, Alice agreed enthusiastically.

'Do you know, I think I'll throw one of my little garden parties very soon. It's so nice to get everyone together now and again. You're very lucky to have found old friends living in the district, Alice, good old Beechonians! Not perhaps the most outstanding of my old girls, but nice enough in their own way.'

Passing the lawn mower, Alice found her eyes drawn to it with a sort of awe. 'There must be a knack to starting it. Do you know how Tom manages to get it going?'

'Tom? Oh he's never managed to get it moving! He brings one of those new-fangled electric things with him.'

Alice got into her car and pulled the door shut with rather more force than was necessary before rapidly executing a turn which brought the vehicle facing her homeward direction, a manoeuvre which clearly surprised Miss Vine. Rolling down her window to wave goodbye, Alice could hear her shout, 'Aren't you taking the books to Barbara?'

Alice, already on the move, called back, 'Tomorrow, I'll give them to her tomorrow!' Glancing in the mirror, she had the satisfaction of seeing an expression of disbelief cross Miss Vine's face as she was confronted with such unaccustomed insubordination.

Soothed by a leisurely bath, wrapped in her silk dressing gown, Alice spooned eggs – scrambled to a creamy nicety – on to toast. Oh the bliss, she told herself, of having only herself to cater for, of no longer feeling obliged to plan and prepare structured meals! Not that she was going to drift into slipshod habits or neglect herself in any way, she assured herself, resisting the temptation to take her plate to the kitchen table and, instead, carrying the tray to the drawing room.

In her grandmother's day, only afternoon tea had ever been served in the drawing room, other meals being taken in either the morning room or the dining room. Now there was no necessity to return to such excessive observance of what was 'correct' but surely now highly inconvenient in terms of housework. Undoubtedly, living on one's own had its compensations. She wondered, briefly, if the fact that she repeatedly found herself dwelling on the delights of solitary living indicated that her contentment with certain aspects of that circumstance might prove to be short-lived and ought to be relished to the full before it waned. She must not allow herself to dwell upon the latter pattern of living in Fernhurst when Sophie had eaten off a tray in the bleak loneliness of that comfortless upstairs room.

She imagined that in time she would yearn to cook 'properly', as she described it. Pouring a cup of tea – Lapsang Souchong, a taste she had rarely felt able to indulge as it had been shared by neither Oliver nor David – she nostalgically visualised herself roasting a leg of lamb, preferably Welsh, spiked with rosemary and garlic; gently folding whipped egg-whites into a lemon soufflé; trickling stock into a raised pie of exquisite symmetry; putting the finishing touches to a walnut cake of perfect texture. Well, she assured herself, it wasn't as though her skills need no longer be exercised. There was no reason why she shouldn't entertain on occasion, but only as and when the spirit moved her, and she would ensure that only those who could appreciate the love and care that went into her culinary skills would be invited to benefit from them.

She wondered how David and Sally were managing now that they were on their own in her tall narrow house in Fulham, and hoped that it was with some difficulty. She suspected, however, that they were managing quite happily according to their own limited standards. Pigging along, she thought, wryly appreciating the aptness of the description.

It had been their sheer lack of appreciation of her care, their failure to realise how fortunate they were in having someone to ensure the smooth running of the household, that she had found so hurtful. She had tried to make allowances, had indeed found something almost endearing in their childish attitude of taking so much for granted. But in time, as she had slowly begun to struggle out of the state of

numbed shock that had followed Oliver's death, their ego-
tistical attitude had begun to irk and, finally, became almost
intolerable. At first, immediately after Oliver's death, it had
seemed such a sensible arrangement for David to return
home, even if it had involved bringing Sally with him. The
suggestion had come initially from David, and Alice, with
hindsight, realised that she had not thought for a moment
about his motives but had assumed without question that he
was solely concerned about her own welfare. Only later had
it occurred to her that they might have had their own interests more at heart than her wellbeing. Sally's flat had been
both cramped and damp. I hadn't been quite myself at the
time, Alice told herself, seeking to excuse her folly as she
recalled the enthusiasm with which she had seized upon
David's proposition. Besides, the years of her marriage to
Oliver had accustomed her to an attitude to life in which the
needs of the other partner were of paramount and mutual
concern and unsurprisingly, as a result, she found it difficult
to grasp the fact that those whom one loved would not
invariably share such an attitude.

Perhaps she had expected too much of David and, with
less justification, of Sally. But surely it had not been unreasonable, she thought – grievance still rankling, feelings still
bruised – to expect at least to be told in advance whether or
not they'd be home for dinner. How else could one shop for
ingredients or cook with the confidence that comes from
knowing that the diners would be present at the appropriate
time? Oh the number of occasions when she'd seen good
food, carefully prepared, go to waste! 'Sorry, but you really
shouldn't have bothered,' they'd say, grabbing a cup of
instant coffee before fleeing to some unspecified engagement
not previously mentioned.

Alice had eventually retaliated by ceasing to prepare
meals for them. They made no comment and had asked for

no explanation. That had been almost insupportable. Without uttering a word of reproach they'd stocked the refrigerator with processed foods and frozen snacks of whose existence Alice had previously only been dimly aware and whose presence in her kitchen she had found deeply offensive.

Thereafter they had rarely sat down in a civilized manner to a meal at a properly laid table but had preferred to graze on lumps of cheese, slices of mass-produced pizza, pots of yoghurt, roughly-hewn sandwiches or sticky pastries. On the frequent occasions when they had forgotten to replenish their stocks, they had been quite content to make do with some revolting package purchased on their homeward journey which they referred to as a takeaway. They'd munch on the hoof or curled up on the sofa watching television or perched on the telephone table conducting long conversations in between bites. Sally would even drink coffee in her bath, leaving her mug on the floor for Alice to retrieve – on one occasion a pickled onion had stared at her from the dregs in a most unnerving fashion.

It had never ceased to amaze Alice how, emerging from the chaos of their room in the morning, Sally contrived to look like the very apotheoses of the competent career woman in sharply tailored suit and immaculate blouse. The day's work over, she would metamorphose into little short of an eyesore: crumpled jeans, one of David's shirts or a voluminous sagging jumper, feet frequently bare and hair like a bird's nest – uncombed since her clothes had been dragged off and then over it.

David had been no better. Well, that was not to be wondered at with Sally for an example! Strange, thought Alice, deftly peeling an orange, how all David's girlfriends' names had started with an 'S': Sally, at least three Sues, Samantha to whom he'd been briefly and disastrously married, Sybil and Selena. There may well have been others of whose existence she had been ignorant. There was quite a lot to be said in favour of ignorance, she thought; the snag was that it did not always reign in the areas which one might choose.

Alice acknowledged that she was fortunate in not having to worry unduly about money but she also realised that she preferred not to dwell upon her recently acquired affluence which, she suspected, had complicated rather than simplified her life.

She wondered if David might show more concern for her if she were not so well protected from material worries. Perhaps she had been misguided in refusing to charge him rent for the house in London; it could be that he saw that gesture as a threat to his independence. The young made such a fuss about independence!

But whatever the reason for David's apparent lack of interest in her well-being, the fact remained that he had only once visited her since she had moved to Fernhurst. While she was still in the process of settling in, he had come down to bring her some things which she had forgotten to pack. He had arrived on a cheerless day in early spring, a blustery wind had blown in from the sea, driving a fine penetrating rain before it so that even the daffodils had flung themselves on the ground in despair. Alice had still been uncertain about the management of the central heating and the pipes had rattled and clanked in rooms uncomfortably chilly. David had mooched about the house seemingly blind to its charms. He had refused to be drawn into a discussion as to the wisdom of her move, had done no more than shrug and declare, 'It's your life, Mother, you must know best what you want to do with it.' Alice had wished she could share his confidence.

Her fingers were trembling a little as she arranged the orange peel in a petal pattern on her plate. What would

Oliver say, if he could see me now, wallowing in resentment, hugging my self-pity? He'd laugh, but not unkindly, and things would slip back into proper proportion. Oh, Oliver . . .

The evening sun patterned the carpet with golden squares, a full-blown rose in the silver bowl on the table at her side shed a petal, then another, and finally in a whispering flurry a little cascade of scented crimson covered the enamelled box that stood on the polished rosewood. Despite Nancy's sensible tidying away, there was no dearth of porcelain figures, table lamps, ivory carvings and assorted *objets d'art* arranged on every available surface. Alice wondered a little at Nancy's resolution in selecting what to remove and pack tidily and carefully out of sight in cupboards and boxes. Alice doubted if she would have the temerity to alter anything, to displace a single object.

The overall effect of so many ornaments could so easily have been one of cluttered confusion, but the wonder was that the room contrived to emanate a sense of peace and order, and certainly not a single discordant note of vulgarity was struck. All was gentle harmony, any colours which might, in closer proximity, have clashed, were discreetly distanced one from the other.

It's a very soothing room, Alice thought, determinedly bringing her wayward mind to bear on the present. The muted colours of the chintzes, the curtains and the carpet, their soft tones of dove grey, lilac, peach and pale green were reminiscent of the inner surface of a shell, fresh from the sea, softly glowing. Alice placed a cushion at her back, and swung her legs up on to the sofa noting with approval as her dressing gown parted that they were still shapely and unblemished. She arranged the periwinkle blue folds of her gown over their nakedness, amused as she instinctively did so at the proprieties the room exacted. Like the shell its colouring suggested, the room cradled her, quietened her mind with promises of peace and security. Lulled, Alice closed her eyes and drifted into sleep.

The light slowly drained from the room, and what time had insidiously, but not yet entirely, stolen away from Alice, the gathering twilight now took from the inanimate objects in the room, softly blurring their beauty, fading their colours, robbing them of the advantage of their imperviousness to the passage of time. Humbled, they must wait for the rising moon to flood the room with its cold milky light and restore their superiority. Long before then, disturbed by the chiming of the little Dresden clock on the mantelshelf, Alice will have awakened in the dusk and taken herself off to bed. The pain of the bleak awareness that now she must retire there alone would be mercifully blunted by the drowsiness of sleep interrupted.

She could at least be grateful that she need no longer lie awake listening for the return of David and Sally, hearing their laughter as they mounted the stairs, perhaps a little tipsy, and the noise of their bedroom door closing behind them, cutting off the sound of their voices. How she had hated herself for the feelings of jealousy that had swept over her, unbidden.

2

'She was jolly miffed!' Alice said in conclusion of her recital of her encounter the day before with Miss Vine. Suspecting that Barbara had not paid much attention to her story, she felt a trifle miffed herself.

'Good for you!' said Barbara, but absently, her mind only too obviously on other things.

Surely, thought Alice, trying not to stare, it is a little bizarre for Barbara to be wearing that rather dressy hat in the house, and at half-past ten in the morning? That hat in any circumstances would look distinctly odd – ruched grosgrain in a peculiarly unbecoming shade of pink. Perhaps if she continued to chat along familiar lines, Barbara would volunteer an explanation.

'I can understand that there are some things that she needs help with, but fetching and returning her library books is something she could surely cope with herself – so why impose on you?'

She could almost see Barbara wrenching her mind away from some private preoccupation to the present.

'I think she likes to keep us toing and froing against the time when perhaps she may become really dependent. It makes her feel safe, knowing that she can just lift the phone

and one or other of us will jump to and do her bidding.
Besides, she's haunted by Beech Park y'know.'

'But she was in her element running Beech Park!'

'No, you don't understand. I mean Beech Park as it is
now – a home for the elderly dotty. Poor old souls who don't
know what day of the week it is, can't even remember their
own names, some of them. You must have seen them, Alice!
Of course they're not so conspicuous in the summer when
we're over-run with such very odd-looking people. But you
can't miss them in the winter when little groups of them are
taken in to Tern Bay for a treat. You see them straggling
along the front in a sort of parody of a school crocodile; but
instead of prefects in charge there are jolly young keepers in
caring specs – you know, the kind that have these huge
owlish lenses. Well, poor old Cornelia is *terrified* of having to
be carted off there one day. Life coming full circle in a grisly
sort of way.'

'Good heavens!' Alice fell silent; it wasn't easy to accept
that Miss Vine might be terrified of anything. Not Miss
Vine, that omnipotent preceptor of the young. She felt
suddenly older.

'Some people do become very strange with age.'

'Yes, I suppose they do,' said Alice, finding the sight of
that hat perched on Barbara's head even more disquieting.

'It's a bit of luck that you came round this morning
because I could do with a bit of help, advice. Let's pop
upstairs and I'll explain.'

'You always had such a good eye, Alice,' Barbara said
over her shoulder as they mounted the stairs. 'I've always
been hopeless at making up my mind and one does get so
out of touch living here . . .'

Alice followed her into a bedroom. The bed was covered
with a foam of tissue paper. Half submerged in its waves, or
cresting its billows, hats were strewn like flotsam. Barbara

waved a hand in the direction of the bed. 'I simply can't afford to buy a new one – have you seen the prices lately? Anyway, one so rarely needs a hat nowadays. I've had most of these for simply years. Jonathan always used to grumble about the space they took up when we had to pack, but I could never bear to throw any of them away. They're a sort of diary.'

She picked up a confection of lavender lace and silk sweet peas. 'This was Joan's wedding. But the thing is, I don't know which one would go best with that,' she said, pointing to a pallid cream-coloured tussore suit suspended on a hanger from the handle of the wardrobe door. 'I bought it at Selfridge's sale when we were up for Freddy's memorial service – which is neither here nor there. It's just that I feel that I have to justify going up to town – Jonathan always makes such a song and dance about it!'

Barbara lifted the pink hat from her head and was leaning over the bed, hand poised uncertainly over one hat and then another.

'Let's see then, what's the occasion – a wedding?' There was a note of hope in Alice's enquiry as they had both reached an age when an invitation to a wedding came as a welcome change to the more frequent summons to a funeral.

'No. The garden party. Oh, not *the* garden party! This one is the annual regimental get-together for retired officers and their wives.'

'That sounds lovely,' said Alice, trying to imagine that great chunk of Barbara's past life as a Service wife.

'No, it isn't at all lovely. It's absolutely bloody! I only go because Jonathan likes it – at least I think he does. Men are rather addicted to reunions, have you noticed?'

Barbara had been trying to smooth down the ruffled feathers on an electric blue skull cap (cocktail parties at the Mess?) and now threw it from her in disgust.

'Honestly, Alice, you can't imagine . . . All that looking back, it's such a mistake. And the gaffes one can make! It's absolutely fatal to ask if so-and-so has turned up this year – because they've either dropped off the perch or have been struck down with something unspeakably awful since last one saw them and there's always someone on hand to fill one in on the ghastly details. That sort of thing takes the sparkle out of the champagne cocktails, I can tell you.'

Hat after hat was impatiently picked up and swiftly tossed aside in disgust.

'And another thing: all one's friends look so *old* – well, none of us is exactly in the first flush, but it's rather unnerving to come bang up against such massed evidence. But some years there's hardly a face I remember and then I see someone vaguely familiar and rush up, all effusive, only to remember a few seconds too late that I'd always positively loathed whoever it is – and it had been mutual. People turn up whom one hasn't seen for yonks and suddenly one realises one has nothing in common any more so one launches into some puerile chat about their children, dredging up names from the sediment in one's memory. Then they gas on about how well their offspring are doing or how many grandchildren they've acquired.'

Suddenly Barbara perched a straw platter crowned with a silk rose on her head. 'And Andrew – how's Andrew getting along? He was such an energetic child, so out-going!' Barbara had adopted a fluting tone, her mouth set in a desperate smile.

She exchanged the straw for a linen cloche and a hunted look. 'Andrew . . . well, we've rather lost touch with Andrew.

'I knew right away that I'd dropped the most frightful clanger! I could see an odious acquaintance who'd been listening in giving me a smug look; later she made a point of taking me on one side and telling me that Jane's Andrew, her white hope, was doing six years for heroin smuggling. Well, how was I to know? Honestly, Alice, that party is about as relaxing as trying to cross a minefield!'

'Come on, Barbara, it can't be *all* bad. I bet there are some old friends there that you enjoy meeting again.'

'Yes, of course one meets real old friends – and I'm not at all sure that that isn't the worst of it, talking over old times and fooling ourselves into thinking that it was only yesterday.'

'Oh for pity's sake, Barbara!' Alice swooped resolutely on the hats. 'Let's eliminate all the ones clearly unsuitable,' she said, briskly tossing the moulting feathered creations, the *jeune-fille* picture hats and the tulle extravaganzas and a couple of sober black funereal numbers to one side. Even in Barbara's salad days none of these could have been considered becoming, she thought. The tussore suit was the wrong colour for her too. Years in hot dry climates had ruined Barbara's pink and white complexion and that washed-out colour was quite unsuited to her now sallow skin. But dear Barbara had never had much taste.

'Where's Jonathan?'

'In the garden. I say, Alice, it's lovely to see how you just *know* what you're doing.'

Barbara had sat down in a creaking basket chair and was watching with admiration as Alice reduced the 'possibles' to three.

'He's out there on the lawn, actually. On duty on his latest project.'

Alice, curious, crossed to the window and glanced out. She was slightly mystified by the sight of Jonathan seated on a canvas chair, a tashed panama sheltering his bald head from the sun, a gun lying across his knees.

'Rabbits?' she asked, tentatively.

'Moles, actually. They started off in the asparagus bed. My dear, he went berserk! He tried broken glass, poisoned worms, exhaust fumes from the lawn mower piped into the runs, planted some foul herb that's supposed to warn them off, even tried Wagner played at full blast on his tape recorder. But nothing seems to work, they keep popping up from time to time. He's convinced they're plotting a pincer movement on the lawn, so he's adopting a new tactic. A sort of heroic last stand.'

'I rather think he's asleep.'

'Probably. That's another advantage of the new tactic; it allows him to do absolutely sweet damn all while claiming to be busy – if you see what I mean.'

'Owzat?' Barbara had risen and tried on one of the hats selected by Alice, a navy-blue boater trimmed with a cream petersham ribbon. 'I've a pair of gloves that'll match the ribbon.'

'Perfect!' said Alice, with more enthusiasm than she felt.

Together they tidied up the discarded hats, replacing them, wrapped in their cocoons of paper, in the card- board boxes that stood in a teetering pile by the dressing table. Barbara, whom the years had thickened and broad- ened, leaned heavily against the bed when they had finished, puffing a little and fanning her face with the boater.

'I really ought to sort things out for jumble, but even when I can bring myself to parting with something I usually discover a use for it later,' she said, replacing the last card- board lid. 'But I have persuaded Jonathan that he's got far too fat for that.' She nodded towards a tweed jacket which hung from a hook behind the bedroom door. 'I'm going to give it to Mary for her Mr Burton. She says she's tired of seeing him in that pinstripe. Although I'd have thought the city style suits him best really, what with his incredibly chiselled features and those hands that look as though they were designed to do nothing more demanding than shell the occasional quail's egg!'

'I don't know how Mary can bear to have him around. I certainly wouldn't give him house room.' Alice gave a little shudder as she recalled Mr Burton's supercilious stare.

'Oh I don't know! You're still new to being without a man about the place – just wait until you've had a bit more of these strange men knocking at the door offering to lop the trees or resurface the drive or asking if you've any antiques to sell, and then perhaps you'll understand how she feels. She did think of keeping a dog, but they can make one more nervous by barking at every little sound, particularly in the middle of the night. No, I think Mr Burton is just right for Mary.' Barbara laughed. 'I did once suggest we'd do a swop, but she didn't seem at all keen. Anyway, I'd rather have Mr Burton around than Tom – now he really is what I'd call a prowler!'

'Tom, a prowler?' Alice asked, startled, trying to visualise Tom, genial helpful Tom, staring through binoculars or peering furtively through uncurtained windows.

'Not a *lurking* sort of prowler. No, the other kind. I mean the sort of man you find wherever there are women who are on their own, have a spot of cash and are getting on a bit. Opportunists who hang around, sniffing the air like stray dogs. Women do like to have a man on call – they can fix tap washers, get rid of wasps' nests, oil hinges – oh, you know the sort of thing I mean. One thing can lead to another. There are still pickings for the Toms – women's lib or no women's lib,' Barbara added, darkly.

Alice, who had been considering imposing upon what she had thought of as Tom's goodwill to remove an old bird's nest from a downspout, decided to brave climbing the ladder herself.

In addition to his skills as a handyman, Tom Beresford provided a focus of enjoyable speculation among his patrons. Well-spoken, good looking and with impeccable manners, he seemed miscast in his humble role. Some said he had been expelled from Public School for taking drugs and had subsequently drifted, ever downwards, as had so many of his contemporaries in the late sixties. Others maintained that he had served a prison sentence and while incarcerated had acquired his multifarious manual skills on a prison rehabilitation course. The sentimentally inclined entertained a theory that a romantic tragedy had blighted Tom's early years and thrown him off course. He lived in a cottage on the wealthy Mrs Cornford's estate. Even the exact nature of his relationship with the widowed Mrs Cornford invited agreeable conjecture. For his part, Tom rebuffed (but with his customary charm) all attempts to probe his past.

'Do stay and have a spot of lunch with me, Alice. Jonathan always goes to The Half Moon on Thursdays when they put on a prawn curry. He'll put those back in the attic later as a sort of peace offering,' said Barbara, indicating the boxes and what state Jonathan might be in on his return.

In the kitchen, Barbara, who belonged to the 'I'm sure I can rustle up something' school of hospitality, poked about optimistically in the cavernous depths of an old-fashioned refrigerator. All that came to light were two singed sausages resting in a saucer of congealed fat, a craggy lump of left-over macaroni cheese, one portion of cold rice pudding and two tomatoes. Barbara declared that the tomatoes with a lettuce from the garden and a tin of sardines would do very well and Alice, who had planned to take herself into Tern Bay for a nice mixed grill at The Lobster Pot, could only agree. Her suggestion that Barbara be her guest at The Lobster Pot had been met with shocked horror by Barbara who declared that 'none of us' ever dreamt of eating out in the village during the holiday season. For four months of the year the people who lived on the Downs behind the village ('on the hill' as they termed it) kept themselves sternly aloof from what they considered the creeping commercial vulgarity that threatened their rural fastness. A weekly, or at most twice weekly, brief sortie was bravely undertaken out of the necessity to buy supplies or visit the bank, but that was all.

They carried their lunch trays to the little octagonal summerhouse at the far end of the lawn. Their voices roused Jonathan from his doze and, giving them an impatient wave, he heaved his bulk out of the chair, shouldered his gun and made for the house.

The summerhouse was hot, its still air stifling. Barbara flung open the windows and the scent of the summer jasmine that clung to the rustic timbers and all but smothered the roof flooded in on the light breeze.

How they had loved this summerhouse as children, thought Alice, remembering other afternoons. All chums together, thin-armed, bare kneed, gingham frocks and giggles. Banana sandwiches, chocolate digestives and home-made lemonade. Four or five little girls fitting easily into the doll house space which now seemed to impose an almost uncomfortable degree of physical intimacy upon herself and Barbara.

'Whatever happened to what's-her-name, we used to call her Monkey?'

'Molly something, had a bit of a stammer. I've no idea where she is now; her family moved away. Sad how one loses touch. Thelma might know; she's the only one of the old crowd who remained put over the years.'

'What decided you, Barbara, to come back here when Jonathan retired from the Army?'

'Daddy left the house to me. We were in Hong Kong when he died. We let it furnished for years, couldn't make up our minds whether or not to sell. Then when we retired it seemed the natural thing to do – to live in it ourselves. Joan was married by then and living in New Zealand. I suppose that if she and Andy had settled in the UK then we'd have bought a house near them to see something of the grandchildren. But it didn't work out that way. So it wasn't really a planned decision to return, it just happened like that. Like most things in life, they seem to just happen!'

Barbara, expressionless, was staring out of the window at a blackbird which was disconsolately pecking at the parched grass. 'You know, Mummy used to say that life was like walking through a series of rooms linked one to the other, and as one door closes, another opens.'

Yes, that would have been the sort of thing Barbara's mother might well have said, thought Alice, who remembered her as a smugly complacent woman of ample proportions. 'Sounds cosy!'

'Yes. We went to Austria for a holiday a few summers ago,' Barbara mused, apparently off at a tangent. 'Somewhere in Steiermark we visited the local tourist attraction – a huge Schloss. We found ourselves herded into a group and were shepherded through endless connecting rooms full of hideous garish baroque and vulgarly awful pictures. It was the sort of place where you had to wear big carpet slipper things over your shoes to protect the parquet. My feet ached, I had a blister on my heel and I could feel my ankles swelling up in the heat. On and on we shuffled, and through the windows we could see the sun on the lovely gardens and the beautiful cool fountains. I can't tell you how we longed to escape from that bloody interminable tour. But we couldn't, you see, because as we were conducted into each successive room, the door behind us was locked and the exit door wasn't unlocked until every drop of tedium had been extracted from the room we were closeted in! Believe me, it wasn't cosy at all. We were simply trapped.'

From somewhere came the noise of a car starting up; Jonathan off for his curry lunch. Barbara was still staring out at the garden with an expression so bleak that Alice turned her head away.

Into the lengthening silence she volunteered, 'Oliver and I used to go to Italy; he loved Florence.'

'We never got round to Italy.' Barbara's voice was matter-of-fact again. 'Mary's told me a lot about Italy; apparently she loved it. She taught English in Rome for a while y'know. She seems to have wandered all over the place, like a gypsy. She's dropped remarks about Sweden, Morocco – even Peru, for goodness' sake! She feeds one little scraps, but one feels that one never hears the whole story. Do you imagine that she collected lovers over the years – even a husband?'

'Goodness knows! Somehow I don't think so. She certainly gathered no moss. I think she just scrapes along financially.' As she spoke, Alice was reminded of a promise she'd made to Mary the last time she had seen her, perched on the seawall with her sketch pad. But she stopped herself from saying more, remembering Miss Vine's talent for extracting information from Barbara, and guessing that Mary would not appreciate Miss Vine learning just how hard-up she was. In their school days, Miss Vine had been fond of predicting a dire future for Mary if she did not knuckle down to work and plan her future. Mary would respond with her good-natured smile. 'Life is not all beer and skittles, my girl!' was the phrase which Miss Vine had surprisingly used. It seemed that Mary had happily enjoyed years of the equivalent of beer and skittles and if, now that she had belatedly settled down, things were not exactly easy for her, she gave no sign of regretting the locust years.

'By the way, Miss Vine tells me she is about to give one of her garden parties,' Alice said, changing the subject.

'Oh hell! That means we'll all be asked to do the work. She writes lists and puts us down for things – last time I was down for four quiches, raspberry mousse and extra garden chairs. She stumped up one pound for the cost of the ingredients – one measly pound, I ask you!'

'Perhaps she's hard-up.'

'Not her! She got a frightfully good price for Beech Park when she sold. Of course some of it went to a couple of the governors who had put money into the school when she first set it up. That rankled, I believe. Originally, you know, she had hoped to run the school in partnership with your Aunt Sophie who was to have bought a fifty-fifty share.'

'I never heard that.'

'No? Thelma told me about it. Apparently your grandfather wouldn't give Sophie the money. Probably didn't want her to be too independent. At the time, of course, they had hopes of her marrying the chap who eventually became Thelma's father, but nothing came of it.'

'Oh yes, I remember hearing something of the sort,' said Alice, who had heard nothing of the kind but felt indignant that Barbara and Thelma apparently knew more about her aunt than she herself did. She dimly recollected Thelma's parents coming to play tennis with Aunt Sophie and her own mother. He had been a big, loud, insensitive type of man, George Dunster; not at all suitable for Sophie.

'Rotten tennis player.'

'Who?'

'Thelma's father.'

'Oh, I didn't know that!' said Barbara, just as though information of equal value had been exchanged.

But, of course, the quality of the tennis played had been neither here nor there. The purpose of these little parties had been to shake Alice's mother back into life; 'to pick up the threads' as Grandmother had put it – as though the death of Alice's father had been a tiresome incident comparable to dropping a stitch in a knitting pattern. No, that was not fair, Alice chided herself, Sophie and Grandmother had, between them, patiently and quietly succeeded in restoring in her mother a resolution to at least continue to live. Lucky mother, thought Alice, the demon of self-pity threatening to materialise.

The soporific torpor that both women could feel creeping over them, weighting their eyelids and slowing their wits, was broken by a wasp buzzing around the cleared plates with such persistence that they were eventually forced to gather up the debris of their meal and leave him feasting, solitary, on a spilt droplet of oil on the table.

Once home, it had been Alice's intention, having remembered her offer to Mary, to go up to the attic and fetch down some of her aunt's old pictures. Part (or for all Alice knew, all) of Mary's precarious income was derived from the sale of her paintings and she had confided to Alice that the price of canvases was now so high that she had had to resort to painting on boards, a method which she found less aesthetically pleasing. It was then that Alice had offered to give her some of Sophie's paintings so that she

could re-use the canvases. Sophie, Alice felt, would not
have been outraged. Her aunt's one and only escape from
home in her youth had been a short spell in Paris ostensi-
bly to practise the language and develop her painting skills.
Her time there might have improved her fluency in French
but had certainly done nothing to further her skills as a
painter – perhaps because they had never existed in the
first place. Sophie must herself have acknowledged this, as
none of her paintings hung on the walls of Fernhurst;
they had never even been framed but lay stacked in mer-
ciful oblivion in the attic. Alice could not remember her
aunt ever touching a brush or even essaying a pencil
sketch.

But the afternoon had vitiated her energy and the
prospect of rummaging in the dust of the attic seemed
singularly unattractive.

Alice set up a deck chair on the lawn but as sleep
threatened to overwhelm her she forced herself to rise
and walk around the garden. Apart from a small vegetable
plot and a modestly sized herbaceous border, the garden
was given over mostly to lawn, a few rose beds and a
thicket of flowering shrubs underplanted with spring
bulbs; a sensible arrangement which reduced maintenance
to a minimum.

It was in the garden where she had so loved to work that
Alice felt most poignantly the presence of Sophie.
Effortlessly, she could conjure up Sophie's outward form:
her figure plump but by no means fat ('comfortable' was the
word that sprung to mind); neat even in her old gardening
clothes but with no suggestion that great thought was
devoted to her appearance; her round face, innocent of
make-up, saved from downright homeliness only by the
shapeliness of her mouth, the liveliness of the expression in
her eyes. But Alice could recall nothing of particular note

voiced by her aunt, no gems of either wit or wisdom to
lodge in the memory of those who had known her. Perhaps
a mark of Sophie's quality was that a woman so apparently
unremarkable had proved to be so memorable. Readier to
laugh than to frown, possessed of warmth, patience and
great kindness, her presence had enhanced the lives of
those around her but not illuminating at all the private preoccupations of Sophie herself. Absorbed with her plants,
head bent over her needlework, never displaying resentment or irritation at interruption – how had her mind been
employed? Surely a woman capable of generating such an
atmosphere of tranquillity and security must herself have
been possessed of an inner core of immense strength cultivated and nurtured as meticulously as the plants that
survived her. It would be foolish indeed to dismiss Sophie
as a pleasant woman but one of no account, of no real
depth. With hindsight, Alice suspected that Sophie's light-
heartedness might well have been born of a realisation that
life was far too grim and serious an undertaking to be
tackled in any other spirit.

Seeing a clump of groundsel under a lilac bush, Alice
stooped to uproot it and discovered in the process an
advancing tide of creeping buttercup. With a handfork
fetched from the garden shed, she was soon absorbed in a
slow and time-consuming progression starting at the edge of
the shrubbery and leading her ever further into its depths.

At last she straightened up, took rueful stock of her dusty
and stained frock and her earth-soiled hands, and wondered, as gardeners will, how the plucking up of one weed
had led to two hours of back-breaking work. Lifting a
branch out of her way and glancing towards the house, she
suddenly halted in shock immobility.

A memory, unbidden, but of awesome clarity possessed
her mind. The phenomenon now so unexpectedly recalled

had, at the time of its occurrence, been so uncanny that in its vivid retrieval she had the sensation that she was reliving the past rather than remembering it. It was as though, for the space of a few seconds, the child of seven and the mature woman that she now was co-existed in the one body. The child of seven stood, as Alice now stood, one arm raised and grasping a branch and seeing the windows of the house blank and suffused with an apricot glow from the rays of the setting sun, the lawn empty but for the one aban- doned deck chair. Now, as then, she was acutely aware of the sweet warm scent of gorse blown on the breeze from the Downs. In her mind was the fearful realisation that the house and garden was forever empty; everyone had myste- riously disappeared and she was alone – utterly and forever alone.

The thin branch snapped in her hand under the pres- sure of her grip and, swaying to retrieve her balance, Alice was securely back in the present and memory, explicable memory, informed her mind. On that summer's day, so long ago, she had scrambled through the shrubbery search- ing for a lost ball, had lifted a branch out of her way and had looked backward towards the house and had then experienced that dreadful moment of . . . of what? Presentiment? Foreboding?

Alice remembered how she had blundered her way through the tangle of the bushes, had run across the shadowed length of deserted lawn screaming with panic.

A window had been flung open; her mother, father and Sophie had come running. Nancy, then a gawky fourteen- year-old, had rushed from the kitchen. It had been Sophie who had reached her first, had scooped her up and carried her bawling and incoherent into the house. Grandfather, making himself heard above the female clamour, had sug- gested, 'Could be an adder bite.' Hands probing, examining.

And, at last, sobs subsiding, flesh confirmed unblemished, safe in the arms of Sophie, the awfulness of her despair had been overcome. But despite the coaxing of the adults she had been quite unable to explain that for one terror-filled moment she had known herself to be alone and in a time when they were no longer there to comfort and hold her close.

3
~

Le Bijou crouched behind a thicket of feathery tamarisk and ragged lilac bushes, an outlandish little bungalow of alien design, built in the thirties at the behest of the widow of a missionary to India. Years of deterioration and neglect had effectively obliterated whatever quaint charm Le Bijou might once have possessed. Around its four sides ran a wooden floored and roofed veranda which robbed of light the little rooms within and the logs stacked along the length of one side suggested that the interior was dank as well as dim.

Alice, who experienced a sense of distaste every time she had occasion to visit it, had come to the conclusion that only its cheapness could have persuaded Mary to make such a horrid little bungalow her retirement home. She had converted the space under the roof into a studio by the simple expedient of having an expanse of tiles removed and replaced with large skylights. It was a conversion which, practical though it might be, had done nothing to improve the outward appearance of the structure. Her funds exhausted by the construction of her attic studio, Mary was obliged to ignore the Estate Agent's injunction that, while the property was one of potential it was undoubtedly 'urgently in need of extensive repair and modernisation'.

Eager to divert the attention of visitors from the sight of rusting window frames and crumbling brickwork, Mary would urge them to share her admiration for the luxuriousness of the Russian vine and the extravagant beauty of the wisteria that between them smothered the sagging veranda roof and twined around its tottering pillars. Suspecting that without their support the whole structure might collapse on their heads, her visitors would fervently echo her appreciation.

Clutching a bundle of her aunt's oil paintings, Alice walked up the path, picking her way between the cushions of saxifrage, aubretia and lemon thyme which all but obliterated the flag stones. Mary, it was understood, believed in generous coexistence with, rather than control of, nature.

The doorknocker, rusted in its hinges, stubbornly resisted Alice's attempts to raise it, only the bolts that secured it to the rotting wood showing an alarming readiness to move in response to her efforts. Noticing that the garage doors gaped open and that Mary's van was absent, Alice gave up her struggle with the knocker and walked round the veranda to the back of the house, the timber flooring creaking ominously under her every step.

She left the canvases at the back door and a nervous glance towards the window of the little dining room afforded a glimpse of Mr Burton seated at the table, one elegant hand supporting his head, the other resting on the page of an open book. He was undoubtedly oblivious of her presence, but Alice drew hastily back and returned to the front of the house by way of the lawn which offered a swifter and more silent route of retreat.

Mary had driven in her van (purchased at a knock-down price from an independent pest controller who had moved on to better things) to Tern Bay. It was there, in the Healthy Country Living Shop, that Alice literally bumped into her.

Mary, her eyes closed, was sniffing ecstatically at an orange pomander cupped in her hands.

'Do have a sniff!' she invited Alice, raising the clove-studded pomander to Alice's nose. 'Isn't that delicious? It reminds me of when I worked in Zanzibar. Oh I do think smells are so evocative! I'm going to buy this to keep the moths out of Mr Burton's clothes – well, that's as good an excuse as any.'

Gripping the pomander's lilac ribbon between her teeth, Mary fished in her pocket for her purse, which she opened with a little flourish, and peeled a note from a slim roll.

'I'm feeling wonderfully flush today,' she said, the pomander paid for and tucked into her pocket. 'I've just sold a batch of watercolours to the souvenir shop down the harbour. "Tern Bay at sunset", "The boats come home", that sort of yuck. With that production stint out of the way and the kitty reasonably healthy, I'm looking forward to indulging myself by painting what I like to paint, which is certainly not what the tourists want to buy!'

Alice told her that she had left the promised canvases at Le Bijou and was rewarded with a spontaneous hug.

Mary was dressed in a loosely fitting frock of Madras cotton which looked as though it might have been run up out of a pair of discarded kitchen curtains (which, in fact, it had – Mary being an enthusiastic bargain-hunter at local jumble sales). On Mary the effect was casually chic. On anyone else, thought Alice, the simple full lines would suggest that fatty bulges were being decently camouflaged, but on Mary's slim body the effect was to exaggerate that youthful suppleness which was so wonderfully preserved.

Alice had intended to visit the antique shop next, but with

Mary still at her side, decided to postpone that pleasure and make the newsagents her next port of call.

They took their places in the queue of jostling visitors recently disgorged from a coach and intent on the purchase of sweets, ice-cream, cigarettes and tabloid newspapers. They waited their turn, Alice clearly impatient, Mary unperturbed and serenely delighting in the sight of so many people dressed in bright holiday clothes and intent upon enjoying themselves.

'Isn't it extraordinary,' she whispered to Alice, 'how English people away from their homes for more than a couple of hours seem obsessed with the need to keep stocked-up on food and drink as though they fear that at any moment they may find themselves in some desert hinterland with not so much as an oasis in sight!' Mary was looking with happy fascination at a stout man at the counter who was paying for a small pyramid of soft drink cans and a large pile of packets of sweets.

But Alice was looking with disapproval at the rack of women's magazines at their side. 'Does it ever occur to you, Mary, that we don't exist?' she remarked, waving at the magazines whose covers, almost without exception, featured young nubile women who grinned coquettishly, pouted sulkily or, clad in leotards, threatened to topple from the page unbalanced by the weight of their thrusting breasts.

'Bit early in the morning for metaphysics, isn't it?'

'Oh you know very well what I mean! When did you last see a woman of our age group – you know, mature but not actually yet decrepit – featured on a magazine cover or in any advertisement for that matter? There must be thousands and thousands of us around, not old enough to be patronised as "game grannies" but not young enough to have our existence acknowledged at all. For heavens sake, even fashion clothes are rarely made in any size above fourteen.'

Alice stopped, realising that that would be no problem for Mary.

'But isn't that just lovely! The young are constantly being told what to wear, what attitudes to adopt if they want to be considered in the swim, what music to go for, even what food and furniture is considered the thing. At our age we are ignored so we can just disappear into the woodwork and get on with living in whatever way we wish. We can do the unexpected and it passes unremarked because there *are* no expectations imposed upon us. My dear, I think it's fabulous!'

'Well, perhaps there's something in that,' but Alice said it grudgingly.

Mary grinned at her, her expression lively, even the harsh fluorescent light failing to deaden the animation in her sunburned face and the intensity of the blue of her eyes.

'Buck up, Alice – don't sound so drumbly! You've been seeing too much of poor old Barbara, I expect. All bloody woe there – and who can blame her with dreary Jonathan and his wretched moles to contend with. Make the most of things, Alice! This is intermission time – remember that by the time we hit our eighties the spotlight'll be back on us and we'll be expected to live up to other people's expectations again and settle for being either dear old things to be cossetted or crochety eccentrics to be patronisingly tolerated. The early warning signs are when people start knitting blankets for you and checking that your flexes don't trail on the carpet. Oh God!'

Alice laughed and wished that she had the opportunity to enjoy Mary's company more often. But Mary was elusive. One came across her by accident rather than by arrangement. Walking on the Downs or on the shore one would sometimes chance upon her, busy with her sketch pad; even then, one would often be greeted with no more than a distant wave.

Alice would sometimes invite Mary for coffee or a meal only to be told that she was about to go up to London for a few days, which she did from time to time, rattling off in her disreputable old van, a few oil paintings in the back which she hoped to place with a gallery.

Alice tried now, tentatively, to extract a promise from Mary to come and visit her soon at Fernhurst but, as ever, in the nicest possible way Mary refused to be pinned down and they parted in the street, each going her separate way.

Alice's way led to the antique shop.

Long before the period when she and her mother had come to live in Fernhurst, there had been the summer holidays, often Easter as well, spent at her grandparents' home and, from as far back as Alice could remember, there had been an antique shop on the corner of Church Lane; its window a treasure house for the curious, its dusty interior a welcome refuge from the rain. In those days it might with greater accuracy have been described as a curio and junk shop. The large bow window had been cluttered with trays of trinkets, odd pieces of china, a scattering of books and a few bundles of sheet music; a variety of bits and pieces accessible to the collector of slender means and, for the shopper less frivolously motivated, a papier mâché tray had displayed a selection of grinning dentures and an assortment of second-hand spectacles. Inside, in dust-moted gloom, pine dressers and mahogany wardrobes had loured down upon the confusion of lesser objects. Ewers and basins had rested on wash-stands topped with marble that resembled slabs of gorgonzola cheese; yellow-handled fish knives and tarnished apostle spoons had clustered in string-bound bundles on little bamboo tables; cake stands, clouded tantalus and clumsy soda siphons had crowded the scratched surfaces of sideboard. Just inside the door, a black majolica pageboy had stood forever guard, proffering

Eva Hanagan

a silver salver on which lay a solitary card which read 'Not for Sale'.

When, shortly after her return to Fernhurst, Alice had seen that the shop still stood, its exterior unchanged, reassuringly familiar in the midst of so much that was unaccustomed and new in the village, she had felt inordinately cheered. Gazing at the tasteful and restrained window-display, she had been rather disappointed to see that the present owner entertained aspirations of a higher order than those of his predecessor.

Curious to discover what changes had been made to the interior of the shop, Alice had entered. The bell which had so entranced her as a child still functioned and rang as she opened the door but the black boy had gone together with the remembered jumble of dusty stock. Having no purchase in mind, Alice had been a little embarrassed to find the shop empty of any other customer and herself the object of the scrutiny of its new owner. Remembering that the cream jug of her Aunt's Crown Derby set was broken, she had made the search for its replacement an excuse for her presence. Although he couldn't immediately satisfy her need he would, he assured her, keep a look-out for a cream jug of the required period to match her set and as he occasionally bought job-lots at house auctions he was quite hopeful of eventual success.

Alice formed the habit of visiting the shop whenever she was in Tern Bay and while the search for the jug had so far proved fruitless, she had come increasingly to enjoy her visits – although she was aware that they were not strictly necessary as Paul Fellowes had promised to telephone her if he did succeed in the quest.

Paul, busy with a prospective purchaser of a Georgian tea caddy, now gave her a welcoming smile and inclined his head in the direction of the back of the shop. Alice walked into the little crowded office at the back where she already felt herself quite at home. She debated as to whether or not she ought to switch on the kettle in preparation for making the coffee which they now drank together as a matter of course on her visits. She decided not to do so, but the decision was made not from fear of appearing to take too much for granted, but because she realised that if the coffee was ready by the time that Paul was free to join her then their chat together would be curtailed by the length of the minutes saved.

It's only natural that I should miss the conversation and company of an agreeable man, she told herself, acknowledging how much these brief visits had come to mean to her. The degree of her disappointment on the days when she found the shop closed was something she did not care to examine fully. Paul had no assistant and, when attending an auction or invited to inspect a piece in situ, had no alternative but to close his shop. But, as he had explained to her, the greater part of his business was conducted by appointment with other dealers rather than by direct sales to customers in his shop.

He had a package in his hands when he joined her, 'So glad you dropped in this morning, Mrs Willoughby! No, no luck with the cream jug yet, I'm afraid,' he added, seeing Alice's expression of simulated pleasure at the possibility that the pretext for her visits had disappeared. 'But I've just bought a small collection of the most beautiful netsuke and I'd love you to see them before the chap I bought them for calls in this afternoon to collect them.'

Alice gazed at the netsuke which were not difficult to admire but, flattered by Paul's assumption that her appreciation might be informed, wisely confined her reaction to a sharp intake of breath and a few words of murmured enthusiasm.

They drank their coffee from Sèvres cups and she listened with unfeigned interest while Paul told her how he had come by the pieces which he now carefully replaced in their box, each piece cocooned in cotton wool. Alice enjoyed watching him do that, his fingers so slim and deft. There was no doubt about it, he was a thoroughly attractive man. Not handsome, at least not in any conventional sense, but with a good, pleasant face whose agreeable expression, she thought, diverted critical attention from a nose that was perhaps less than aquiline and a mouth that was a trifle too large for the fine bone structure of jaw and brow. His dark hair was receding and revealed more than a trace of grey, but in a man of . . . what? late forties, early fifties possibly, that was only to be expected. But it was his voice that particularly captivated Alice; it had a warmth, a certain timbre that reminded her irresistibly of Oliver.

When the bell on the street door jingled, Alice declined his invitation to 'hang on a mo!' Although Paul always seemed genuinely pleased to see her, she was fearful of outstaying her welcome and, perish the thought, eventually being regarded as a tiresome caller who took up his time and interrupted his work.

On the homeward stretch of lane that wound up and away from the sea and the village, Alice found herself driving slowly, more alive than she had been on her outward journey to the fragile beauty of the dog roses that trailed over the hedges, the lacy froth of the cowparsley that covered the verges.

Not until she had reached the gates of Fernhurst did Alice realise that for the past few minutes she had been filled with unalloyed delight. Her pleasure was unmarred by any feeling of anguish that Oliver could never again enjoy such moments of simple enchantment, of sudden glad consciousness of the sheer delight of being alive. She waited for guilt to assail her, but was aware only of its absence.

Perhaps, she reflected, they had not been so foolish, those well-meaning friends who had persisted in assuring her that time does heal, that eventually even the terrible pain of irrevocable loss would ease and that the ache that would succeed it would prove to be both manageable and not necessarily continuous.

I'm a little bit further on, she thought, and longed to tell someone of her progress but then wryly acknowledged that perhaps only Oliver would have been genuinely interested.

4
~

It promised to be a perfect day for Miss Vine's garden party. Alice had risen early and started work while long shadows still lingered on the lawn outside and the kitchen itself had seemed chillingly unfamiliar, being not yet roused from the stillness of the night when no intruder had disturbed its silence. Alice found herself deliberately imposing her presence upon the quiet: humming to herself, clattering utensils in the sink, closing doors and drawers with firm deliberation. Now she flung the kitchen window open wide to dispel the heat and the odours of cooking, and the breath of the garden that drifted in was almost as warm as the air within but heavy with the fragrance of phlox and roses.

She surveyed with satisfaction the end product of her labours which, on plates and wire trays, covered the kitchen table. Had she had the option, Alice would have preferred to be entrusted with the roasting of the chickens or the baking of the quiches which were to form the main ingredients of the party meal. But Miss Vine, in marshalling her labour force, had assigned to Alice what she had airily dismissed as the preparation of 'bits and pieces'. The detailed instructions that had followed had made it clear that the provision of a few bowls of crisps and nuts was not what Miss Vine had in mind.

Alice poured herself a glass of sherry and took it to the open kitchen door where she squatted on the doorstep to await the arrival of Mary who had volunteered to collect the conscripted helpers' contributions in her van; an arrangement which Alice, not without a touch of envy, considered an easy option on Mary's part.

Fanning herself with a cardboard plate, Alice idly watched a hen chaffinch on the lawn busily stuffing grubs down the gullets of a late brood of fledglings. She always felt a concern for the birds in spring and early summer; their endless frenetic activity of nest-building and chick-rearing was so exhausting even to observe. It seemed unjust that by the time the last of their offspring reached independence the parents would be too weary to rejoice in their own freedom but, worn-out, would instead retreat into sullen moult and barely retrieve their energy and *joie de vivre* before the hardships of winter were upon them.

When Mary arrived, sprightly and cool-looking, she carried under one arm a picture which she placed with a flourish upon Alice's knees.

'A little presie in return for the canvases.'

Alice stared, baffled, at the picture.

The canvas was dominated by what appeared at first glance to be a square but was, in fact, not quite an equilateral figure; it was placed off-centre and coloured bright red. Smaller squares and rectangles painted in grey, primary yellow and blue, and seemingly randomly scattered, filled the remainder of the space and all were separated one from the other by thick straight black lines. The effect was stark and somehow shocking.

'Goodness! How interesting . . . so very unexpected, really most unusual!'

'Don't you recognise the genre?'

'One of those cubist things, isn't it? Thingummy – that Dutch chap?' Alice hazarded, a vague memory stirring of some television programme – or had it been an article in one of the Sunday colour supplements?

'You're getting warm. But it's not cubist. It's a pastiche of Piet Mondrian and he wasn't simply a cubist – he was, well, Mondrian, a one and only!'

That at least was a comfort, thought Alice. 'It looks very clever,' she said, raising her eyes from the picture; staring too long at these vivid primary colours and black lines was something, she felt, best avoided. Mary looked radiantly excited, but it occurred to Alice that it could have been the effort of wrestling with the steering of her decrepit old van that had occasioned such a heightening of her colour.

'It was all rather extraordinary – how I came to paint it.' Mary had seated herself on the doorstep beside Alice, knees drawn up, hands clasped tightly round them.

Alice, recalling monologues which had been inflicted upon her by an aspiring poet with whom David had enjoyed a mercifully brief flirtation, surmised that she was about to be subjected to the ordeal of the artist explaining her source of inspiration. Resigned, she assumed an expression which was designed to suggest sympathetic interest and to convey as much encouragement as would not seem discourteous but would not be so generous as to prolong the experience beyond the bounds of her endurance.

'Remember that I told you I'd just finished churning out a batch of popular pap? Horses looking over gates, boats bobbing about in the harbour, seagulls wheeling over cliffs – that sort of thing. Well, I was looking for some way to exorcise my mind – to clear my palate, if you'll forgive the pun! I was looking at that canvas with your aunt's awful flower thing and, I suppose because it had been painted around

1922 and in Paris, it made me think about Mondrian's early work — you know, those frightful dying chrysanths and sunflowers. Thinking about that phase in his work led to me thinking about what he was painting in the twenties when he'd at last discovered his true style — not, of course, that what he had started doing gained any approval at the time.

'It may sound crazy, but suddenly I felt I just knew why he'd felt impelled to develop the style of painting that he did and I felt myself in sympathy with the aversion he'd developed towards nature. Only temporarily in sympathy, if you understand me; a bit like the way the very thought of a chocolate can make one feel positively ill if one has been guzzling too many. I had this terrific urge to paint something that had none of myself in it, something devoid of sentiment and subjectivity . . . oh hell, how can I put it? I felt a need to commit a sort of act of hygiene! Do you follow what I mean?'

'Well . . .'Alice murmured tentatively, but Mary wasn't really waiting for an answer.

'You see, too much of the sort of painting I have to do in order to bring in some cash eventually blunts the painter's perceptions. There comes a point when one needs to break away from habit and routine because, otherwise, one is no longer seeing what is *really* there. Not, of course, that one ever totally succeeds in seeing anything — or anyone for that matter — as it actually is because things are always blurred by one's own subjective approach. That goes for everything, not just what we see in a visual sense.'

'You mean that we see what we want to see?'

Mary, who had been staring at the middle distance, now glanced towards Alice with an expression of exasperation. '*No!* Well, perhaps. Yes, I suppose there is that too. But there's more to it than that. OK, we may see what we want to see but, equally, we may see what we dread to see because everything that we bring to our vision reflects our own flaws, our lack of certainty, our fears, our meanness – oh, the whole caboodle that we hump around.'

Alice decided that to allow the silence to lengthen might be the best strategy. The doorstep was beginning to strike through her frock with awful chill. Perhaps Mary was beginning to suffer the same discomfort, because abruptly she scrambled to her feet, strode a few yards on to the path, and, sounding a trifle defensive, declared, 'Well, that's about it. I went ahead and painted that picture in Mondrian language and it really did me good. I felt cleansed, purged, as though I'd been on a fast or swallowed a huge dose of salts.'

'As you say, how very extraordinary!' Alice glanced again at the picture on her lap and tried to imagine its execution in purgative terms.

'I was so carried away that I was tempted to put "P.M." in the corner – but I decided that would be gilding the lily!'

Alice, hoping that she didn't sound ungracious, suggested that as painting the picture had had such a miraculous effect upon Mary then she must surely want to keep it for herself. Alice, for her part, would be quite content with one of her more conventional paintings instead, one of the harbour would really do very nicely.

But Mary was adamant. If it had not been for Alice's gift of the canvases, she would have been denied the immense therapeutic benefit of painting the picture. It was only fair that Alice should have the painting. 'Besides,' she added, 'I'm sure you'll get quite a bit of fun out of seeing people think that you have a genuine Mondrian!'

'Yes, there is that.' Alice wondered how many of her acquaintances were likely to have heard of this Mondrian fellow, far less go into raptures over one of his paintings – fake or genuine. Most likely they'd think the kindest thing to do (were she foolish enough to expose Mary's picture to view) would be to pretend not to notice it at all, and that wouldn't be easy.

To her embarrassment, Mary flung her arms wide, gave a little skip and then grasped Alice in a sudden bear hug.

'Oh Alice, I really do feel on top of the world! I've been taking a good look at my life and I think it's time to make a change. Things are suddenly resolving themselves in my mind – just like that,' she said, clicking her fingers, 'D'you know the feeling?'

Alice made noises of understanding, thinking it best to humour Mary while she was in this odd euphoric mood. Perhaps she was 'on something'; there was a lot of that sort of thing about. Well, it would be little wonder if Mary needed a little something to tide her over when her natural optimism flagged. Poor Mary, always short of cash, living in Le Bijou with only Mr Burton for company. Suddenly protective, she took Mary's arm and guided her back to the open door.

'What about a glass of sherry – or would you prefer a gin and something?'

'Thanks, but I'd better not. I already had a gin with Barbara who was in a bit of a tizz – well, you can imagine. But I wouldn't say no to a squash – it's so damned hot!'

In the kitchen, Mary gazed with gratifying admiration at the laden table where a miniature forest of cocktail sticks impaled a variety of morsels and crowded ranks of *petits choux* and canapés bore testimony to the hours of fussy work that had been imposed upon Alice.

'That lot must have taken you simply ages!'

Alice shrugged, 'Well, it isn't as though I haven't the time . . .' That, she thought, was too sadly true. The days of summer were slipping away, one almost indistinguishable from another and each equally aimless. The Old Beechonians had entertained one another: a dinner party here, a coffee morning there. There had been walks on the Downs, a little gardening, housework, shopping – and always the feeling that she was putting in time, waiting for life to present her with a purpose. Barbara was right, one was trapped until the Guide chose to unlock the next door. But she suspected that life wasn't like that for Mary who had the air of one who was equipped with her own set of skeleton keys.

Alice propped the picture up on the kitchen dresser and, stepping back, gave it an appraising look. 'I do believe, Mary, that you could start up a very nice line in forgery if you had a mind to. It must be wonderful to have such talent.' Mary's return to a more rational manner called for some reward.

Mary nodded, unabashed. 'Yes. Sometimes I wonder if I should have done more with it. But I'm not cut out for all that pompous stuff about a duty to serve art and so forth. I've made my talent serve me – give me the freedom to live as I choose. I've been lucky too, one way and another.'

Mary moved the picture slightly so that the angle of the light was altered. 'I must say I'm quite pleased with it. But I can't tell you how relieved I was that your aunt's work was so absolutely ghastly! I'd have had a conscience about painting over work that was reasonably good but, as it is, I feel that I'm giving a sort of decent burial to daubs that cry out for just that. If you ask me, your Aunt Sophie must have had a streak of masochism in her to have even kept them! What rather puzzles me is why your grandparents thought it worth forking out to send her to Paris when she so obviously had no talent at all for painting.'

'Well, I suppose there was the language too. I think she was sent to one of those genteel little places where they took English girls and coached them in French, took them to concerts and arranged classes for them in this and that – you know the sort of thing.' But, when Alice came to think about it, Sophie at twenty-two must have been a little old for the conventional 'finishing' process.

'Mmm,' said Mary, helping herself absentmindedly to a vol-au-vent, 'perhaps she'd been sent off to get over an unsuitable attachment. She never did marry, did she, your Aunt Sophie?'

Mary was a fine one to talk, thought Alice. Racketing around the world for years, fancy free – although, of course, one could not be absolutely sure of that.

Reading her thoughts, perhaps, Mary continued, 'Oh I know, not everyone wants to get married but for our generation it's usually a considered decision, whether or not to get married, because we have options. But when your Aunt Sophie was 'a gel' it was the main be-all and end-all – or so we are led to believe.'

'But, Mary, don't forget, there was a terrific shortage of men after the Great War. There were masses of spinsters around when Sophie's generation was young, and they certainly had not all remained unmarried from choice. Anyway, we'll never know now why Sophie stayed single.' Alice started to gather up some of the trays from the table. 'Let's get this stuff into the van or we'll have Miss Vine ringing me up.'

She felt defensive about Sophie. It seemed disloyal to even listen to Mary speculating about her. It was, after all, none of Mary's business. An 'unsuitable attachment', Mary had suggested. Alice had never thought of Sophie in the light of suitors, unsuitable or otherwise. Sophie had just been Sophie, always there, the dependable and loving aunt. And that, thought Alice, everything at last packed into Mary's van and Mary waving goodbye, is surely the way she would have wished me to think of her. Sophie's generation had not felt the need to endlessly discuss their private lives with others. A reticence, thought Alice, which had a great deal to commend it.

I wonder how on earth it could have given Mary such pleasure to paint that, thought Alice, looking in some puzzlement at the picture on the dresser. It seemed a pity that Mary should have parted with it, and to have given the picture to someone like herself who had no liking for geometric abstraction was even more unfortunate. Alice wondered if, even had she been knowledgeable about his work, she would have realised that it was not a genuine Mondrian. It was only too easy to mistake the imitation for the genuine and, for that matter, vice versa. Wasn't that what Mary had been on about? Well, something like that.

Suddenly irritated by the deceptively forthright and uncomplicated statement of the picture and its strong pure shapes and brash colours, she snatched it up and carried it to the larder where she stood it, face to the wall, behind the collection of empty Kilner jars which awaited disposal at the next church jumble sale.

Miss Vine's garden, the heat trapped between its high beech hedges, was very warm and very full of people, few of whom Alice recognised. Food was set out on trestle tables and Miss Vine herself stood behind a large terracotta urn from which she was dispensing a cloudy concoction liberally laced with chopped fruit. Dressed in a long flowered kaftan and crowned with a broad-brimmed leghorn straw hat of ancient vintage, she flourished a large soup-ladle with an almost regal air and a fine disregard for the driblets that bespattered the white sheet covering the trestle. Barbara, whose bed-linen it was, looked less sanguine.

Thelma was purposefully stomping down the garden pulling behind her at the end of a length of binder twine a dejected dachshund. Alice caught up with her, feeling less conspicuous in her company than standing alone on the edge of the chattering groups of strangers.

'Had to bring Binky with me. She's on heat and I daren't let her out of my sight. Poor old girl, she hates crowds. I'm looking for a bit of shade to tie her up in. This'll do,' she said. They had stopped in the shadow of a damson tree; in the long grass below it a heavy lawn roller peacefully rusted its days away. Thelma stooped, stocky legs wide-splayed, and tied the improvised lead securely to the iron handle of the roller.

'Nobody'll disturb her down here,' she declared, straightening up and sniffing the air which was rank with an odour that made the panting Binky sit up straighter and look almost happy. 'Cesspit's in bad shape,' she added, casting a diagnostic glance towards a tangle of brambles and nettles behind the tree. 'Toby offered her a dead sheep – but she didn't take him up on it. Stubborn old bat! Nothing like a carcase dropped into a cesspit to get the bacteria going!'

'Is Toby with you?' Alice asked when they felt it was safe to slacken their pace and amble more companionably beside the neglected herbaceous bed where nicotiana spilt its heady scent on the still air.

'No. There's a cow that he's worried about. At least that's his excuse – can't say I blame him.'

'Look at that!' Thelma was pointing to some wilting pelargonia and a clump of lobelia which had been carelessly heeled into the soil. 'It's just as I suspected – that urn that she's using for the wine-cup is the one that usually stands by her back door full of plants; I thought there was something familiar about it.'

'Who are all these people?' Alice asked, throwing her drink over the plants and then bending to flick away the evidence of glistening blackcurrants and banana slices that had come to rest on the lobelia.

'Mostly Old Beechonians who come toadying in from all over the place. Quite a contingent come down from London by train. Younger vintage than our crowd, most of them. Thank God none of them live near enough to put in more than an annual appearance – pretty ghastly crew. They're the ones who subscribe to that beastly Old Girls' news mag thing that Miss Vine fills up so much time with. If you ask me, they're all a bit retarded!'

Alice wished that Thelma would keep her voice down a little. 'Well, at least it's made her happy – she looks as though she's really enjoying herself.' Alice having purposely spoken quietly had to repeat her remark more loudly and Thelma then took it as a reproach.

'And so she jolly well ought! The only work she's done herself is to concoct that foul drink. And it's more lethal than you might think – she lets it brew for days. You'll see!' Thelma's expression held a certain gleeful malice as her eyes roved over the guests whose behaviour seemed to Alice to be positively staid – at least, as yet, she thought, perking up a little at the prospect of something livelier to come.

'It's the following day that it really hits one,' Thelma added, dashing Alice's hopes.

'Look! There's old Lauder still going strong – well, perhaps not, but still going anyway. She's staying overnight with Miss Vine. Echoes of the past, what?'

Alice, remembering the ebullient Miss Lauder who had taught biology and taken netball, looked with shocked compassion at the shrunken little figure with the pronounced dowager's hump and pathetically stick-like legs whom Thelma was pointing out to her. Old age has simply nothing to commend it, she thought, conscious of a sudden stab of fear.

Thelma was laughing. 'Thank God I grew up on a farm! Remember her little talks on "the more intimate aspects of life"? They'd have been just fine if we'd been frogs or buttercups!'

Alice did remember. She also remembered that Thelma had been eager to impart more pertinent enlightenment in exchange for half a crown. She had picked the lock of her money-box but later wished that she had been content with Miss Lauder's ambiguous dissertation which had at least had the advantage of not being frighteningly disgusting.

Their gaze in Miss Lauder's direction caught the attention of a couple at her side who now started to walk towards Alice and Thelma.

'Hell! I'd better see how Binky's getting on.' Thelma turned away and, in defiance of the heat, broke into a little run, leaving Alice to face Clare, with Desmond in tow, bearing down upon her with determinedly bright smiles.

'Well, well, well, how nice to see you again, Alice!' Desmond was jerking his hands up and down in a ridiculous fashion, a sandwich in one and a glass in the other preventing him from rubbing them together as was his wont.

Clare, once and forever the 'swot' of the form, had qualified as a teacher and married a colleague. Both retired now, they kept their intellects alive – or so they claimed – by reading the *Guardian* and both attending and conducting adult education classes every winter. In the coming session, as they went to some lengths to explain to Alice, Desmond was to conduct a study of D. H. Lawrence and Clare was to attend a series of lectures on the birth and significance of the Co-operative Movement.

I'm sure they're really a very worthy, well-meaning couple, Alice scolded herself after she had at last persuaded them that they really must go and look at Thelma's dear little dog.

There were now fewer people around the buffet and Miss Vine appeared to have grown unaccountably taller. Moving closer, Alice could see that she was standing on a box, the better to reach with her ladle to the bottom of the urn. Alice poured some home-made lemonade from a jug, virtuously declining the glass of wine proffered by Miss Vine on the grounds that she had already had her share and wouldn't dream of depriving someone less fortunate.

'Isn't the afternoon going well, Alice dear!' said Miss Vine. 'Everybody having such fun!' she declared, scanning her guests from her advantageous height.

'Is Tom here?' Alice asked for want of anything else to say.

'Tom? Don't mention that fellow to me – he promised to help and then reneged when he thought he had better fish to fry. Not that one should be surprised; he has his uses but he's not quite a gentleman. Not that *she* would be expected to detect that.'

'She?'

'That vulgar Polly Cornford woman.' Miss Vine leaned forward and took a swipe with the ladle at a passing wasp. 'She's gone off to the West Indies for a holiday – money no object, of course – and she's taken the perfidious Tom with her. The man's got no pride, tagging along like a puppy dog, all expenses paid. Oh botheration!' Miss Vine had dropped her ladle into the urn and was now crossly trying to retrieve it, plunging her arm in to above her elbow.

'Allow me!' Alice turned at the sound of the familiar voice and was surprised to see Paul standing behind her in the company of Mary. A quick tilt of the urn, a shake, and he had rescued the ladle.

'Oh, very masterful!' Mary murmured and before Alice could do more than smile at Paul, Mary had taken her by the elbow and led her away from the table.

'I've been looking everywhere for you! Come and meet some of the other guests; you can make up your mind which of the London lot you would least resent having to run to the station when our hostess starts organising departures.'

'Barbara warned me about that – so I left the car at home and walked here.'

'I always knew there was more to you than a pretty face!' Paul had followed close behind them, and although she knew the remark was no more than a threadbare cliché she felt girlishly pleased. Perhaps something of that reaction showed in her face because Paul continued. 'You know, I've been having quite an amusing time listening to all the feminine chat. Do you realise that when speaking to one another you all lapse into the sort of expressions and slang that were current when you were at school together?' He nodded in the direction of a group of younger women at a little distance. 'Now that lot, for instance, employ a slightly different idiom from the women clustered round the vicar; I would guess that they left Beech Park circa 1945.'

'When was your sister at Beech Park?' Mary asked, incidentally satisfying Alice's curiosity as to Paul's acquaintance with Miss Vine.

'Oh, some time in the fifties.'

'Is she here today?' Alice asked, hoping the topic of dating and implicit categorising by age group might be dropped.

'Good Lord, no! No, Camilla married and then they took themselves off to the U.S. of A.'

Alice allowed herself to be propelled in the direction of one group after another. Somewhere along the way Paul detached himself from their company and she glimpsed him talking to Jonathan and wondered if their conversation could possibly be less boring than those to which she was being successively subjected, but thought it unlikely. Paul, head slightly inclined, was listening with every sign of polite attention. Didn't Barbara contend that Jonathan was interested in discussing only his mole vendetta, cricket or the state of his liver? Which of these topics could have so captivated Paul's attention, or was this simply further evidence of what she already believed, that he was an exceptionally kind and considerate man?

The air in the garden was becoming more stifling, the light more sulphurous and a glance at the sky showed violet-hued clouds banking over the Downs. The chatter became subdued, even the wasps pillaging the debris of the buffet were infected by languor, more and more falling to Miss Vine's counter-attack with a decrepit table-tennis bat.

What the devil am I doing here? Alice asked herself. She felt sticky and weary and her ankles were beginning to swell.

Thelma's shout, cleaving loud and clear through the glutinous air, broke the somnolent spell.

'Binky's slipped her bloody collar!'

Before her startled guests could guess what was about to befall them, Miss Vine was among them, waving her arms like a demented traffic policeman as she energetically organised search parties to locate the errant Binky.

Alice decided that this was the moment to make her departure even though it meant slipping away without the conventional leave-taking of her hostess. I can always telephone later and made my apologies, she assured herself, slinking quietly away. Gaining the front of the cottage, safely out of sight and lengthening her stride, she was dismayed to hear footsteps on the path behind her.

She turned guiltily, a hasty fabrication about an impending migraine, 'the thunder in the air, y'know' already under construction in her mind. It was Paul who had followed her.

'Another defector!' he said, forestalling her excuse with a conspiratorial grin. 'Let me give you a lift home; my car is in the lane. Come on, if you start walking you'll only get caught in the rain; it's going to bucket down any moment now. Hear that?' A faint but unmistakable mutter of thunder was carried on a sudden puff of cool breeze.

Opening the car door for her, Paul suggested that unless she was in a great hurry to return to Fernhurst they should go for a quick drink. Alice, who felt quite depressingly sober, assured him that she was in no haste to get home; indeed that was only too true. The lone return to an empty house after a party, the bleak knowledge that there was no one with whom she could conduct a post-mortem on the shared experience was something to which Alice had not yet adjusted herself; she doubted if she ever would.

The drive to the small country pub that Paul had in mind was a short one but it was soon evident that he could not, perhaps would not, indulge in the pleasant pastime of sharing a little blithe gossip about the recently shared entertainment (if that was the right word). Alice stifled a sigh of disappointment and resigned herself to making noises of politic agreement as he sang the praise of Cornelia Vine (a woman of sterling and lovable character) and Barbara's Jonathan who was described in tones of affection as a 'fascinating old buffer'. Could Paul possibly be so benignly tolerant and good-natured, or was he simply exercising laudable discretion? It had been Alice's experience that men who were prepared to exercise a little goodwill and effort could equal, if not excel, women in the exchange of amusing and uncharitable comments upon mutual friends and acquaintances.

Well, one must not expect too much too soon, she told herself, seated in the pub and enjoying her gin and tonic while listening with mild interest to an informative little talk on the merits and origins of the landlord's collection of old pewter, some of which had been purchased from Paul. It pleased her that he now addressed her as 'Alice'; a small thing of itself, perhaps, in these days of informality, but comforting for all that.

After her second, or it could have been her third, drink, Alice could think of few things that could be more agreeable than just sitting there in the soft light listening to Paul's beautiful voice and finding herself the object of someone's – anyone's – exclusive attention. It occurred to her, as Paul pointed out various structural features which he said were evidence that the building had originally been a small Elizabethan Manor house, that he was possibly unused to entertaining women tête-à-tête; that too seemed an amusing and agreeable circumstance.

The pub began to fill up with other customers, young people shaking the rain from their anoraks and talking in loud confident voices. Paul paid them not the slightest bit of notice, his glance straying to neither the young women nor, as Alice cautiously observed, their fit and energetic young men.

By the time they took their leave, the short, fierce thunderstorm had blown itself out, the macadamed car park was as jet and shiny as liquorice and the air, freed from the oppression of the sultry day, was fresh and light with a tang of the sea behind it.

'I could do with a coffee; what about you?' They had arrived at Fernhurst and Alice was clambering out of the low-slung car in some haste before Paul could open the door for her and witness an emergence which might appear less youthfully executed than she would wish.

He followed her through the hall and into the kitchen where there lingered a faint and appetising intimation of the morning's activities – a whiff of chopped basil, the tang of lemon and the slightest suggestion of garlic. Thank God I decided on chicken liver and not kipper pâté, thought Alice.

She set mugs and the biscuit barrel on the kitchen table, rejecting the idea of coffee in the drawing room as being inappropriately formal.

Alice was recounting some of her memories of Tern Bay before it had become a popular resort (and not omitting to mention that she had been *very* young at the time) when she broke off to remark that she'd quite forgotten to put out any sugar.

'No, do go on, I'll fetch it,' said Paul as she started to get up.

He'd brought the bowl of demerara from the cupboard and they had both helped themselves from it before the implication of his action was borne upon her. 'How did you know where the sugar was kept?'

For a moment Paul looked as dumbfounded, as disconcerted, as herself. Then he recovered himself, smiled disarmingly and spread wide his hands as though, in the manner of a conjuror, he were demonstrating that there were no cards up his sleeve.

'I simply can't tell you! I wasn't consciously thinking about it . . . it was just, well . . . involuntary.'

'But how very extraordinary! Has anything like that ever happened to you before – you know, finding that you know something although you couldn't reasonably have been expected to know it?'

Paul shrugged. 'Well . . .' he began, uncertainly, 'I can't recall anything off-hand. But I imagine that if we put our minds to it, we could all recall strange occurrences for which we can't find a sensible answer. Telepathy perhaps . . . well, who knows?'

For a few seconds they both stared at the sugar-bowl as though it might volunteer an explanation.

Alice was tempted to confide in him her disconcerting experience in the garden when time had apparently not

conformed to the accepted rules. But the implications were
too intimate, too painful to voice; too disturbing, indeed,
for herself to dwell upon them. In a muddled and confused
way the two incidents seemed, to her mind, to share a
significance, even a connection.

Her common sense asserting itself, a prosaic explanation
of Paul's action presented itself to her. 'Did you know my
Aunt Sophie – ever visit her here, I mean?'

Paul shook his head. 'No, I never met your aunt. But, of
course, I knew of her. She and Miss Vine knew one another
and she's spoken of her to me more than once. Wonderful
person, I understand, your Aunt Sophie.'

Alice nodded and, distracted from the immediate mys-
tery, began to tell Paul about Sophie. His interest seemed
genuine and, encouraged by his quiet attention, she found
herself pouring out her feelings of guilt over the way in
which she had neglected to keep an eye on her aunt's welfare during the last years of her life. In mitigation, she
described the pressure that had been placed upon both her
time and nervous energy by Oliver's long terminal illness.
She found herself able to talk about Oliver and the near-
despair into which his death had flung her.

Paul was certainly an ideal listener: sympathetic, grave
when appropriate and not given to voicing trite or banal
phrases of comfort. Nor did he attempt to distract her by
any account of personal misfortune – an irritating response
previously encountered by Alice on the rare occasions when
she had felt driven to confide her grief or self-doubts to
another.

Later, when he had taken his leave and she was replacing
the sugar-bowl in the cupboard, Alice realised that they
had arrived at no reasonable explanation of his knowledge of
exactly where it was habitually kept and that the subject
had, in fact, been side-stepped. Surely what had happened

had some mystical significance? At the very least it indicated that there existed a psychic sympathy between Paul and herself. I wonder . . . she thought, taking the bowl from the shelf and holding it cupped in her hands, its rotundity smooth and cool against her flesh.

Oliver would have liked Paul, she decided, gently replacing the bowl and closing the cupboard door.

5

~

She was certainly ravenous, this comical cat who, ignoring Alice, had walked past her through the back door. Tail carried high – a disproportionately long tail, curled over at the top like a handle – she had walked purposefully across the kitchen and stopped in the corner by the dresser. Only then did she turn her head and favour Alice with a rather imperious stare. She glanced down at the empty floorspace and turned again towards Alice and this time her unwinking stare was accompanied by an impatient miaow. Closing the door, all thought of the chives which she had been about to fetch for the omelette she planned to make for her evening meal dismissed, Alice opened a tin of sardines and mashed the contents into a saucer which she placed in front of the cat. The cat rewarded her with a chirrup and a quick rub of her head against Alice's leg before directing her full attention to the food.

Long-legged, dappled in black, amber and white, the cat, in common with all tortoiseshell and whites, was certainly female. Alice was almost equally certain that she had been Sophie's cat as this was the type of which Sophie, a confirmed cat lover, had been particularly fond. How could I have forgotten that there had always been a cat at

Fernhurst? Alice rebuked herself, adding another item of
self-reproach to her list. She watched this last in the long
line of Sophie's cats as the saucer was methodically licked
and polished clean. Apologising for her lack of prescience,
she hastily placed a second saucer brimming with milk
before the cat. She accepted it as no more than her due.

Replete, the cat strolled through the kitchen into the hall
and with one white-tipped paw pushed wide the half-opened
door of the drawing room. From a respectful distance, Alice
watched as the cat leapt lightly on to a cushioned armchair
and settled down to a fastidious and leisurely grooming with
a nonchalance which suggested that an accustomed routine
had been resumed with a gracious forgiveness towards those
responsible for its temporary suspension. Aware of Alice's
gaze, the cat paused, pink tongue protruding slightly, and
met her eyes with a look which Alice interpreted as being
benignly dismissive. Tactfully she withdrew, leaving the cat
in undisputed possession of what she clearly regarded as her
territory.

Nancy must have taken her with her when she had left
Fernhurst. Had the cat subsequently found her way back
from wherever Nancy now lived? Although hungry, the cat
bore no signs of having undertaken a long trek to reach her
old home. Perhaps, thought Alice, when she had moved
from Tern Bay Nancy had left the cat behind with her sister. Now she really would have to seek out Nancy's sister, if
only to confirm that the cat was indeed Aunt Sophie's and
to let her know that it had returned to Fernhurst where she
was perfectly happy to allow it to remain provided that that
met with Maud's agreement. She felt almost relieved that
the visit which she had for so long cravenly postponed was
now being forced upon her.

With the benefit of hindsight she felt that, despite the
solicitor's advice, she ought to have visited Nancy as soon

as she had been fully acquainted with the provisions of Sophie's will. She had spoken briefly to Nancy at the funeral and had learned then that she was living in her sister's house in the village. But not until the following day, when she had kept an appointment with the solicitor, had she learned with surprise of the lack of provision for Nancy in Sophie's will. If Mr Appleyard had known Sophie's reason for such apparently heartless treatment of Nancy, it was clear that he had no intention of divulging it. Alice's immediate reaction had been one of angry indignation, and she had insisted that, in order that Nancy's long service to both her grandmother and her aunt be acknowledged, she wished then and there to make arrangements for an annuity to be purchased from a share of her own inheritance so that Nancy would at least be adequately provided for.

But Mr Appleyard, plump pink hands folded on his blotter, silver-rimmed spectacles perched on the end of his nose the better to gaze at her earnestly with his pale and rheumy eyes, had counselled caution. Her aunt, he had said, had written to him expressing clearly the change which she had wished to make to her existing will, a change which had involved cancelling the legacy that she had previously wished to leave to Nancy. As instructed, he had attended her at Fernhurst a few days later with the new will and was accompanied by his secretary in order that the signature might be witnessed. Miss Cutler, he said, although bedridden and physically disabled, had been perfectly lucid and neither he nor his secretary had any reason to think that she had not been perfectly aware of what she was doing. Her aunt had also given him to understand that Nancy had been informed of the purpose of their visit and the nature of the alteration to the original will. Nancy, for her part, had betrayed neither rancour nor distress, so one could only assume that she both understood and accepted as fair her employer's decision.

It would be unwise, nay (the word was Mr Appleyard's) even intrusive, for Alice to enter into discussion of the matter with Nancy.

Could it be, Alice had ventured (although finding it difficult to believe her aunt capable of such financial sophistication), that Sophie had made a material gift – some part of her grandfather's collection, perhaps – to Nancy with a view to avoiding estate tax?

Mr Appleyard had primly replied that if that had indeed been the case then he had not been privy to the transaction and would not care to speculate upon such a supposition.

Alice, anxious to return as quickly as possible to Oliver, had postponed making any decisions as to what she ought to do. Later, physically exhausted, her nervous energy depleted by Oliver's illness and death and the recent stress occasioned by the death of Sophie, and still trying to grasp the implications of the change in her material circumstances consequent upon her inheritance, Alice had meekly capitulated to Mr Appleyard's persuasive plea that she should 'leave well alone'.

Her decision to uproot herself and move to Fernhurst rather than sell the property had also been made while she was still in a bemused state and not entirely capable of rational judgment. But I don't think that that decision was wholly mistaken, Alice reflected, looking back upon her actions with an objectivity born of her recently acquired happier emotional state.

But my motives were certainly confused, she thought, acknowledging that she had had some muddled and possibly foolish notion that by returning to a place which she had known as a child and a house which, in some ways, she regarded as 'home', she would somehow recover the self-sufficiency of youth. Coming home to Fernhurst, she had believed, would impress upon her that she had once been happy in an existence in which Oliver had played no part and that realisation might in some way restore her ability to face life on her own. Alice could not, as yet, decide whether or not that belief would prove to have been well-founded.

But her weak-kneed decision to 'leave well alone' in the matter of Nancy was a different thing altogether. She had definitely been wrong in taking no action, of that she had been convinced for some time. But when she had eventually arrived at this conclusion Nancy was no longer living in Tern Bay. Nancy had, in fact, left the village just a few days before Alice had moved into Fernhurst. It was not surprising really because Nancy and her sister Maud had never got on well together. Sophie had been well aware that there had been no love lost between the sisters. Surely her aunt had not fully realised that by so shamefully depriving poor Nancy of the legacy that was surely no more than her due, she had also thrown her on the charity of the awful Maud.

Alice could remember Sophie telling her, with some amusement, that Maud had been 'affronted' by Nancy's acceptance of a domestic post at Fernhurst. Their father had owned what was recognised as the best grocery shop in the area, serving not only the better-off residents of Tern Bay but also customers of discrimination from a large part of the surrounding countryside. It was Maud's opinion that, as the daughter of such a high-class grocer, Nancy ought to have regarded herself as being above such menial work and might also have considered the humiliation it inflicted upon her sister, who entertained a higher estimation of her family's social position in the community.

Maud's own position in the family shop had certainly, in one sense at least, been an elevated one. Alice could remember seeing her seated in a sort of minstrels' gallery high up at the back of the shop from where she controlled the little canisters of money which whizzed to and fro on overhead cables between the counters and her cash box. When not occupied with controlling the aerial cash flow, Maud would stare crossly down upon the lesser mortals below like a plump goddess impatient for further propitiation.

Alice had enjoyed accompanying her aunt or her grandmother on visits to that shop. The air within was redolent with the smell of freshly roasted coffee beans, the pungency of fine cheeses, a faint spiking of spices and the round full scent of ripe fruit. Glass-lidded tins ranged in front of the counters displayed a confusing variety of biscuits and the solid mahogany counters above supported pyramids of epicurean delights: elegant glass jars of ginger in syrup, plump pheasants in aspic, boxes of chocolates, little wooden caskets of crystallised fruits and marrons glacés, honey in the comb, drums of turkish delight and sticky dates in boxes on whose labels camels took their ease under exotic palms. The more mundane comestibles were ranged in packets, tins and jars along the shelves which rose from floor to ceiling behind the counters.

The guardian of this Aladdin's cave of gastronomic treasure was Mr Dutton whose gleaming white jacket buttoned tightly across a bulk that was itself a tribute to the nourishing properties of his stock. His florid face (a trifle porcine, it is true) was garnished with a magnificent waxed moustache which, so local legend had it, was protected within a little cage when its owner laid his head to rest at night. So smugly did his indelible pencil rest between his right ear and his bald skull, so closely did his thick pink fingers resemble his best quality sausages, that one might be tempted to believe that Mr Dutton had been specifically designed by nature for no other occupation than the one he so devoutly pursued.

Somewhere in the store room at the back, sugar, flour and dried fruits were bagged, butter was sliced from golden slabs, weighed and packeted or, if it was the customer's fancy, patted into rounds and imprinted with a pattern of corn sheaves. It was there in the back shop, out of sight of the customers, that Nancy started work when she left school, and if additional duties had not from time to time been imposed upon her, she might never have come to the notice of the family at Fernhurst at all.

In answer to an after-hours telephoned request by Cook, Nancy would sometimes be dispatched on her bicycle to Fernhurst with some ingredient omitted from the order but now urgently required. It was on one of these missions that Nancy had been recruited to replace the then living-in maid who, in the tiresome manner of domestic staff, was faced with the necessity of getting married as quickly as could be arranged.

Sophie, recounting to Alice the circumstances of the household's acquisition of its subsequently irreplaceable treasure, had recalled even the detail that it was an ounce of angelica which had brought Nancy cycling through the rain on a November evening to the back door of Fernhurst. Smitten by conscience, perhaps, Cook had invited Nancy in for some warmth and a cup of tea and it was there in the kitchen that Sophie had first seen her when she had entered with some last minute instruction for Cook.

Looking like some Dickensian waif, Nancy was perched on the edge of a chair and steaming gently in front of the range. Her hands, red with the cold, were cupped round a mug of tea and her feet in their muddy galoshes rested on a newspaper. Cook had popped her damp gloves in the warming oven and draped her dripping mac and sou'wester over a clothes horse. Unprepossessing the scene might have been, but it did not prevent Sophie from detecting some special quality in the bedraggled Nancy. Sophie 'just knew that Nancy's future lay in Fernhurst'; that was the phrase that she used when explaining her flash of intuitive insight to Alice.

Weary, perhaps, of deputising for the errand boy, Nancy had accepted the offer of employment at Fernhurst and after a brief tussle, and despite Maud's protests, Mr Dutton had been persuaded to give his consent. A widower since Nancy's birth, Mr Dutton was probably relieved at the prospect of having his family responsibilities halved.

The breach between Nancy and Maud had remained open. Maud married a man whom Nancy described as 'travelling in custard and jam' – it was hardly surprising that a man so colourfully presented had caught even the lofty Maud's attention! Maud's Percy eventually joined his father-in-law's business and when old Mr Dutton was eventually called away to the great emporium in the sky, Nancy did not seem either surprised or particularly upset that it was Maud and Percy who inherited the shop.

The manner of Mr Dutton's death had been both dramatic and regrettably public. Mrs Cutler had been unfortunate enough to witness it. One moment he had been standing on a pair of steps reaching up for two tins of asparagus tips and the next he was swaying and groaning in a most alarming fashion and then, before Mrs Cutler's shocked gaze, he had suddenly crashed to the floor, cracking his bald pate on the edge of the mahogany counter on his way. Her finely honed sense of what was, or was not 'done' had prevented Mrs Cutler in the ensuing confusion from laying claim to the tins of asparagus, which was a pity because they had been the last of his pre-war stock.

The war robbed Fernhurst of Cook – not in any heroic sense; she had simply left in order to run a canteen for off-duty soldiers. But Nancy remained. She anticipated conscription for war work by joining the Land Army and was sent to work at a nearby farm while still living at Fernhurst. It was not, from Mrs Cutler's point of view, an entirely satisfactory arrangement but, as she pluckily expressed it, 'better half a loaf than no bread at all!'

Before leaving the house at an uncomfortably early hour in order to present herself at the farm in time for the morning milking, Nancy attended to the range, set the breakfast table and put the porridge on to simmer at the back of the stove. When the draining away of the daylight put an end to her work on the farm, Nancy would return in time to help with the preparation of dinner, or, according to the season of the year, to a meal which had been considerately kept warm for her in the oven and to a sink stacked with dirty dishes. Mrs Cutler maintained that this routine preserved Nancy's self-respect and left her with no undue feeling of obligation about accepting free board and lodging – a debt which such work as Nancy could reasonably accomplish on her day off from the farm would have scarcely discharged.

The farmer was evidently satisfied with Nancy's work and 'little perks' came her way from time to time. Now and again she would be rewarded with a chunk of mutton – the sheep had grown very accident-prone during the war years. On occasion a fowl too old to lay would be brought home to enliven the Fernhurst menu and there were the eggs too, sometimes as many as three at a time! Mrs Cutler was particularly appreciative of the eggs because when she was suffering from one of her migraines she declared that the only form of nourishment she could tolerate was a lightly boiled freshly-laid egg.

Although deprived of the attentions she had become accustomed to from Sophie who now spent her days doing voluntary work at the hospital, Mrs Cutler felt that she could lay claim to the proud boast of having obeyed the injunction of 'business as usual' throughout the ordeal of the war. Even her migraines had been turned to advantage, her affliction sparing her from the imposition of evacuees. Her doctor had committed his opinion, and in writing, to the billeting officer that Mrs Cutler's nervous condition could not withstand an ordeal of that nature.

By the time the war ended, Nancy's footing with her employers had undergone a subtle change. She became more deeply absorbed into the family. True, she continued to eat on her own in the kitchen and there was no question of her sitting of an evening with Mrs Cutler and Sophie, but the advent of television was to change even that.

Mrs Cutler, at Sophie's suggestion, decided that there could be no harm in inviting Nancy to join in watching, on occasion, a programme of historical significance, such as the Coronation and Churchill's funeral. The definition of what was improving and educational was gradually extended to include natural history programmes and a carefully selected few which purported to increase the viewer's appreciation of cultural matters.

While the Victorian observance of family prayers might have inculcated a laudable awareness of brotherhood in Christ between employers and servants, the corporate worship of the small screen in the morning room of Fernhurst brought about a slackening of the bonds of formality and the danger of a degree of secular levelling which must surely have exceeded Mrs Cutler's original intention. But this loosening of the bonds of convention was achieved so unobtrusively, so insidiously, that a new and more intimate relationship had been irrevocably established before

Mrs Cutler, Sophie or Nancy had fully realised what was happening.

When Mrs Cutler did become aware that Nancy's role had changed from that of domestic help to one that could better be described as companion-help, she became vigilant in her search for evidence that Nancy might take advantage of the situation. But Nancy never did overstep the mark, her perception of what was correct being as acute as her employer's. Mrs Cutler felt that her faith in her Jesuitic assertion that, provided she was caught young enough, a girl could be perfectly trained to acquire all the attributes of a good servant had been fully justified.

It really is appalling, thought Alice, beating eggs with unnecessary vigour, that at the end of the day Nancy should still be driven to work for her living – and at her age! I really ought to have put things to rights before this, she thought, wondering if there would ever be an end to self-reproach.

She reminded herself that she had made more than one attempt to write to Nancy but had invariably failed to finish the letter. She shrank from further wounding Nancy's pride and self-respect, and perhaps too conscious of the danger, found it difficult to arrive at a wording that was not implicitly patronising or critical of her aunt's strange action. Besides, how could she, without appearing to be accusatory, frame the questions she wanted to ask as to how her aunt had come to spend the last months of her life in such bleak and spartan surroundings?

A talk, face to face with Nancy, surely offered the best solution. But while Mr Appleyard had grudgingly offered to forward any letter she might choose to write to Nancy, he had not felt free to entrust her with Nancy's address, postulating that that might constitute 'a breach of confidence'. He took the view that as Nancy had failed to communicate with Alice one could not rule out the assumption that she would prefer her whereabouts not to be revealed to Alice. Maud, Alice could only hope, might prove more forthcoming and she could then visit Nancy unannounced and avoid altogether the difficulty posed by the writing of a letter.

Carrying her supper-tray into the drawing room, Alice found the sight of the cat asleep in the chair opposite her own surprisingly comforting. Maud will be able to tell me her name, she thought, trying to find something agreeable to look forward to as part of the outcome of tomorrow's visit.

6
~

She would do her shopping before bearding Maud, Alice decided, adding 'lemon' and 'spinach' to her shopping list. Wiener schnitzel, creamed spinach and potato salad was what she planned for the main course for that evening's dinner with Paul. She didn't need to concern herself about what they would drink with the meal as he always brought a bottle of wine with him, saying that it was the least he could do in return for the hospitality which she had extended to him over the past few weeks.

The opportunity (and Alice freely admitted to herself that she did see it as that) for her to entertain Paul so frequently had arisen from his decision to redecorate his flat above the antique shop. His first step had been to call in a builder to carry out a few minor alterations, but his inspection had revealed rotten floor-boards, defective electric wiring, an infestation of woodworm in the roof timbers, something radically wrong with the plumbing and a long list of other faults all requiring immediate attention. Faced with such devastating domestic upheaval, Paul had needed little persuasion to avail himself of Alice's offer that he should dine at Fernhurst as frequently as he pleased.

The cat followed Alice as she left the kitchen and got

ready to go out. As she drove away, Alice saw that the cat had settled herself contentedly on the sunny back doorstep and was watching her provider's departure with an air of placidity, suggesting that she would patiently await Alice's return when she would expect to be rewarded with a share of the spoils of her hunting expedition.

Taking her place in the queue at the butchers, Alice saw that the customer who was dithering over the rival merits of rump steak as opposed to chump chops was Barbara. To the relief of the waiting customers, she finally made up her mind and settled for two portions of steak, specifying one large and one small.

Recognising Alice as she was leaving the shop, Barbara seized her by the arm. 'Alice! What luck to see you, I was going to phone, but things have been at sixes and sevens – I suppose you have heard?'

Alice shook her head, hoping that whatever it was that she was about to be told would not take so long in the telling as to jeopardise her place in the queue.

'Jonathan shot himself!'

Seeing Alice's look of shock, Barbara hastily added, 'Oh, only in the foot!'

Did she detect a note of regret? Alice wondered, but hastily dismissed the thought before it might take root. 'My dear! How absolutely awful. When?'

'Day before yesterday. Very early in the morning, actually. The mole vendetta, you know. He'd started a dawn patrol campaign. Slipped on the wet grass, he said, but I guess he was a bit squiffed; he'd been up all night afraid he'd miss the first light, having the occasional tipple to keep himself going – well, you know what Jonathan is like!'

'How is he?'

'Well, his foot's a bit of a mess as you may imagine, but the hospital reckon they'll patch it up O.K. But I think they

may keep him in for some time. You know how it is – you
go in with one thing and then they start poking around and
making tests and before you know where you are they've
discovered umpteen other things. It's like putting the car in
for a service – one always ends up with a thumping great
bill for a new exhaust, tyres, the lot! Thank God Jonathan's
in a National Health bed.'

'I'll tell you what,' said Alice, conscious of the avid interest of the other customers and nobly abandoning her plans
for a refreshing afternoon rest before entertaining Paul, 'I'll
pop in this afternoon to see you and we can have a proper
chat.'

'No, don't do that! What I mean is, well . . . it'd be
lovely, of course, but I have to go to visit him this afternoon,
you see.'

'Of course, silly me! I'll ring you later.'

'Fine! Must rush, I've left the car parked on a double
line.'

Parcelling up the veal fillet and the liver for the cat, the
butcher remarked that Mrs Frobisher had left the bacon
she'd bought on the counter. Alice, guessing that he hoped
she'd offer to do so (and not loath to hear more about
Jonathan's accident), picked up the parcel and said she'd
deliver it on her way home.

Although the grocery shop had long since disappeared (converted into an amusement arcade), the Dutton family house
had survived the changes that had overtaken Tern Bay. It
was a substantial Victorian villa of forbidding aspect; the
railway track lay at the end of its back garden and the bow
windows at the front looked out upon the sea.

A straggle of sweet-williams and pansies cowered behind
the low brick wall that separated the narrow strip of front
border from the pavement. A 'Bed and Breakfast' card was

propped in front of the net curtains in one of the windows.
Alice had heard that Maud's husband had taken a more personal interest in the licensed department of the shop's trade
than had been prudent and by the time of his death Maud
had discovered herself to be not as comfortably provided for
as she had expected.

The door was opened by Maud herself, essentially
unchanged since last seen by Alice. Stouter certainly, her hair
now sparse, iron-grey and scraped back into a tight bun,
Maud still looked out upon the world with an expression of
impatient disdain.

'Oh, I heard you were back!' was her greeting – although
her dour acknowledgement of Alice's presence on her
doorstep scarcely warranted such a festive description. She
opened the door a little wider and stood aside, an action
which Alice interpreted as an invitation to enter.

The white-painted narrow hall had an air of scoured,
stark cleanliness which struck the visitor like a gust of icy
air. The sole decoration on the bleak walls was a wrought
iron trough filled with scarlet plastic geraniums, as visually
startling as a stain of fresh blood on a bandage. There was a
faint smell of pine disinfectant and, in a wild flight of fancy,
Alice could imagine Maud plying an unspeakable trade with
a knitting needle in the service of women in trouble.

Maud showed her into a little sitting room at the back of
the house. In contrast to the hall, this room was dark, the
light struggling through the dusty branches of a monkey-
puzzle tree which did not quite succeed in hiding the
railway track. Alice averted her eyes from the horsehair-
stuffed leather sofa below the window which fitted only too
well into her unpleasant fantasy. Maud waved her to an
upright chair and seated herself on the opposite side of the
brown glazed fireplace whose cold grate was filled with a
dark green crêpe-paper fan.

Alice launched into the story of the cat. Maud listened impassively and without interjection, so that Alice heard herself gabbling nervously, elaborating unnecessarily.

Alice could well believe that this house was cleaned with the aid of bass brooms and wet tea leaves, scrubbing brushes and yellow bar soap, but as she paused (hoping that Maud might say something – anything) she could hear a vacuum cleaner humming in the room above. Maud inclined her head slightly, as though supervising the unseen worker from a distance.

'So I thought . . .' Alice continued, hesitant now in the face of Maud's lack of encouragement. 'Well, I'd come and see you, and you could tell me if it actually is my aunt's cat. I wondered, too, if you might be worried about it – I mean, if it had been living with you and then just wandered away.'

Maud broke her silence. 'Yes, that'll be April right enough.'

'Is that her name? April, what a lovely name, very unusual – at least for a cat!'

'Always thought it was a daft name, myself. Something to do with it being pied, or so Nancy said. Doesn't make sense to me, that. Nancy brought it with her when she moved in here, but she had to leave it behind when she left, the lady she went to work for not being partial to cats. It wandered off once or twice when Nancy had gone, but with Fernhurst being empty it used to come back. Must have had another go and decided to stay when it found you there.'

'Do you think . . . would you like me to bring her back to you?'

'Why ever would you do that?' You keep it, and welcome. After all, it's nothing to do with me! I told Nancy she should have had it put down by rights. Nothing but trouble, cats. It's not your responsibility, I said to her, no reason why you should take on the bother and the cost of feeding it. She paid no heed, of course. But she was always too soft, Nancy was. Always one to be put upon.'

'We were all very fond of Nancy. I don't know how my aunt would have managed without her.'

'You never said a truer word! And I suppose that's why she was left penniless – after slaving her life away for that lot up at Fernhurst! Not that she told me all the ins and outs of it; well, she wouldn't, would she? Didn't want to give me the satisfaction, after her flying in the face of my advice. But you can't tell me she would've gone off to a job at her age if she didn't have to. Crying disgrace, I call it!

'Mark my words, if she'd stayed in the shop where she belonged, there's no saying where she might have ended up. We've all seen where a start in her father's grocery shop can lead a girl – haven't we?'

Alice nodded, there being no gainsaying that.

Maud leaned forward, her fingers splayed on her broad Crimplene-covered knees. 'I told her right from the start that she ought never to have gone to work at Fernhurst. But there was no reasoning with her. There's no doubt in my mind that it was all your Aunt Sophie's doing – she bewitched her, that's what! Slaved her life away for her, Nancy did. More fool her! But she's my sister, when all's said and done, and no one can point the finger at me and say I didn't do my duty for my own flesh and blood. I can hold my head up in that respect – and there's many as can't. "Nancy," I said, "what's happened to you, you brought on your own head. But I'll let bygones be bygones; there's no good crying over spilt milk." And then I told her she could make her home with me. Any road, it's not as if any of us is getting younger and I won't deny that an extra pair of hands was a help. But after a month or two, she was up and off.

'I should've guessed that there was something up when she started buying The Lady.' Maud snorted. 'The Lady indeed! Bit late for that sort of caper, I said, seeing as how you chose to spend your life as a skivvy! But it was the ads she was after, you see.'

'Where did she go?'

'Somewhere up near Buxton. An elderly lady who wanted someone as a paid companion-help: able to drive, good plain cook and fond of the country – oh, and dogs,' said Maud, as though reciting the wording of the advertisement.

'I didn't know that Nancy could drive.'

'Your Aunt taught her. Pleased as Punch, Nancy was at the time. But I said to her, "if you ask me, it's only so as you'll be more use to her ladyship. You'll see!" And I was right. After your aunt was struck down, it was handy for her that Nancy could take her around in the car; as long as she was able to go out, that was. Later, of course, she just kept to her bed. But you wouldn't know about that, would you, you not being one for coming to see your aunt all that much. Still,' Maud raised a fat hand as though to ward off Alice's protest although in fact, Alice sat mute, 'no doubt you had your reasons. It's not for me to criticise. At the end of the day, we're all answerable to God, and it's for Him to judge!'

Alice sat, her eyes not meeting Maud's, her hands clasped tightly in her lap. In a strange masochistic way she almost welcomed Maud's vilification. Half an hour in the presence of this malevolent woman was as good a penance as the wearing of a hair-shirt for a week.

'Do you think you could let me have Nancy's address? I'd like to get in touch with her.'

'I have it somewhere – although she's not a great one for letters. Probably doesn't get the time. I warned her that, for all that the advertisement said, it'd just be another skivvy

job dressed up with a fancy description to sound posher.
"Companion-help" indeed! But the pay was to be better
than anything she ever got at Fernhurst – not that that
would be difficult! I told her straight when I met her out
shopping one day, your aunt being bed-ridden by then, that
she should see she got her due with all the extra work she
had to do. Tell your Miss Sophie, I said, that our Lord
Himself said that the labourer is worthy of his hire. All that
running up and down stairs! I know what it's like to look
after someone who's bedridden. I had my share when my
Percy was taken bad with his liver, and under the doctor
until the day he was taken. God rest his soul. There should
have been a proper trained nurse engaged to look after your
aunt, not just poor Nancy dancing attendance.'

'I'm sure there's a lot in what you say. That's why I'd
like to see Nancy, to put things straight.'

'Put things straight! It's a bit late in the day for that.
Still, if it's a case of you wanting to see Nancy, well you'll
get your chance when she comes down here on a visit.'

'She's coming here?'

'And why shouldn't she? There's some who know what
family obligation is, if you don't mind me pointing it out.
Nancy's coming down to see me for the last fortnight in
September, D.V. Her employer's niece is going to stand in
to let her off for a bit of a holiday. Very considerate, I'm
sure.' Maud looked smugly pleased with this last sally.

'Good. I'll be in touch when Nancy makes her visit,' said
Alice, rising.

Maud, her face a little flushed with the triumph of
having, as she would have put it, got so much off her
chest, saw Alice to the door and wished her good-day with
a veneer of affability more objectionable to Alice than the
spiteful diatribe which had preceeded it.

*

Barbara's car was parked outside her front door and Barbara herself was topping up the radiator as Alice drove up.

'I seem to have caught you just in time!' Alice remarked. Having explained about the parcel left at the butchers, she was presenting it to Barbara with the basket of fruit that she had bought for Jonathan.

'Actually, I'm not leaving until after lunch but I'm just giving the car the once-over – it's really quite a long drive to the hospital.' Barbara had evidently been checking the oil level and now began to wipe her hands on a grubby rag.

Seeing the state of Barbara's outstretched hands, Alice retained her hold on her gift to Jonathan.

'I'll just put these in the kitchen for you,' she volunteered and, ignoring Barbara's protests that she needn't bother, walked ahead of her through the open front door.

One end of the kitchen table was set for lunch – luncheon for two, as Alice noticed. That explained the steak. There was a beer glass by one setting. That was interesting.

Barbara was busy scrubbing her hands at the sink while she gave Alice details of the extent of Jonathan's injuries. The fruit in the basket had become a little disarrayed and after Alice had rearranged it to her satisfaction, she raised her eyes and looked in Barbara's direction. Through the window she could see a man perched on a ladder, clipping the yew hedge at the far end of the garden.

'Goodness, isn't he brown!' she remarked, admiring the bare muscled shoulders and wondering if it would appear too inquisitive if she slipped on her long-distance spectacles to get a clearer view of that shirtless torso. 'He's certainly more attractive to look at than my old Fred – not that he'll even go up a ladder! What with his rheumatism and his dizzy turns, he's not much use, really. But I haven't the heart to replace him.'

'Could you just hand me that towel, dear,' asked Barbara, edging Alice rather clumsily away from her stance in front of the window. 'Had a letter from Joan today.' Barbara plucked an envelope from her pocket. 'Of course she won't have had mine yet about her father's accident. Makes it difficult – her being so far away. She sent some photos of the children. Isn't Annabel a sweet child?' she asked, thrusting a photograph under Alice's nose. 'And this is little Jenny. Once she stops having to wear that brace on her teeth, I think she'll be rather a beauty – so like Joan at that age!' Barbara was holding up a second print just out of Alice's reach.

She's acting like someone manoeuvring a pony with a sugar lump, thought Alice. 'Mmm, they're lovely . . .' she murmured, side-stepping Barbara and returning to the window as though seeking a stronger light on the photograph already in her hand.

'Barbara,' she said, staring hard at the distant figure, 'that's Tom, isn't it?'

'Clipping the hedge, you mean? Yes, you're right, it is Tom.'

'After everything you said! Really, Barbara.'

'What did I say?' Barbara met Alice's scandalised look with an expression so ingenuous as to sting Alice into indignant reaction.

'You know perfectly well what I mean! You said Tom was a "prowler" – something to the effect that you wouldn't have him near you.'

'Did I say that?' Barbara glanced away from Alice's accusatory glare. 'Well, yes, perhaps I did – and perhaps he is. But I really don't see what you're making such a song and dance about.'

'But what's he doing here, anyway? I thought he was spending the whole summer with Polly Cornford somewhere in the West Indies. "Tagging along like a puppy dog" was how Miss Vine described it.'

'Well, he's come back home, hasn't he? Polly Cornford treated him appallingly! Seems she picked up some young man in the hotel and turned absolutely beastly towards poor Tom, so, of course, he had no option but to come home. Besides, he couldn't have afforded to go on staying there if he had to pay the bills himself.'

'Serves him jolly well right, then.'

'Oh Alice, that's not fair! I don't know why people are so nasty about him – it's not as if there's any *harm* in Tom, not if one doesn't allow him to take advantage of one. If you don't mind me saying so, Alice, you don't seem to have changed much since we were children – you always were a bit "pi", you know.'

'Oh no, I wasn't!' Alice snapped.

'Come off it, dear, you certainly were.'

'That's not fair! You were the one who always sucked up to the mistresses at school – you're still doing it with Miss Vine.'

They glared at one another for a few seconds and then Barbara broke the tension with a giggle. 'Isn't this all a bit ridiculous? Don't let's fall out, Alice, it's all really too silly! Sit down, do, and I'll get us both a drink. Gin and something?'

'Sorry, Barbara.' Alice tried not to sound grudging, but being "got at" twice in one morning was rather too much. 'Of course what you get up to is none of my business.'

'Not to worry!' Barbara patted her hand briefly as she placed their drinks on the table. 'If old friends can't snap at one another from time to time, it would be a poor look out.'

Barbara sat herself down at the table. 'I've got Tom's measure, don't you fear! Anyway, I'm grateful to have him coping with this and that in the garden and it'll be a great relief to Jonathan to find everything in good order when he is allowed home. I doubt if he'll be able to do much in the garden for some time.' She swirled her drink around in her glass and added, 'There are lots of things Tom can do that are beyond poor Jonathan.'

Alice suspected that that was probably only too true.

'And he really has had a very shabby deal from that ghastly Cornford woman.' There was a little silence as they finished their drinks. When Alice spoke, her tone was ruminatory, as though she were doing no more than thinking aloud.

'Hadn't he let his cottage to holiday-makers for the summer? That must be awkward for him.'

'Yes, that too. All his arrangements gone to pot!' Barbara hastily pushed back her chair, glanced at her watch and picked up their empty glasses. 'Must get my skates on, dear, if I'm to leave on time for the hospital. The ward sister's a frightful dragon – terribly good for Jonathan! But I must give Tom his lunch before I go. Least I can do,' she added.

Alice stood up and glanced at the parcel of bacon (with its connotations of breakfast) that still lay on the table. 'Better get that in the fridge; it's been sweating in the boot of my car for too long as it is.'

Barbara swept it up. 'Thanks awfully for bringing it, Alice. Bacon's so handy for little snacks! You know how it is when one is alone – all the customary routine seems to slip away. But there's a lot to be said,' she added, closing the refrigerator door on the bacon, 'for making the best of it really. Getting out of the rut and, well, just having a little bit of something tasty when the fancy takes one, when the opportunity presents itself, as it were!'

Barbara smiled, her eyes very bright, but that, Alice thought, might just be the gin. 'Of course it's a bit different for you, I know. When being left on one's own isn't just a temporary condition, then I suppose one feels a need to return to something more permanent and conventional. One has to think about the long-term situation – am I right?'

'Yes, I expect so,' replied Alice as off-handedly as she was able, being a little confused as to whether or not it was regularity of meals that was under discussion.

7
~

The Stilton, its condition of ripeness beyond criticism, had been placed on the table and the dishes which had preceded it had been as perfectly prepared and presented as Alice's exacting standards demanded. Dinner had reached the stage when Alice felt she could comfortably relax and devote her full attention to her guest.

Paul had, as always, protested that she went to far too much trouble on his behalf and, while not denying that careful thought and work went into her cooking, Alice was at pains to assure him that she genuinely enjoyed exercising her skills for someone as appreciative as himself. Nothing would have annoyed her more than to be told by a recipient of her hospitality that he would have been equally content with macaroni cheese or something on toast. Paul, fortunately, was unlikely ever to commit such a solecism.

In the course of previous conversations, she had learned that Paul's mother had been French and that, as a consequence, he had spent some time in France. Alice, who had little personal knowledge of the French, was pleased to believe that it was these genetic and cultural influences that had endowed Paul with his tact and charm and, naturally, his appreciation of fine cuisine.

His wife, Paul had told her, had also been French. Alice, while commiserating with him over the tragic circumstance of her death in a motorway accident a scant eighteen months after their wedding, could not help privately regretting that death, and not divorce, had terminated his marriage. A dead spouse, particularly one who had scarcely been granted time to display normal human failings, could be worshipped in a fashion that left any subsequent female friend at a distinct disadvantage.

Alice had once ventured to observe that when a marriage had been ended by death, the happier it had been the more likely it was that the survivor would seek another partner in the hope that such happiness might be experienced again. While agreeing with her supposition, Paul had laughingly added that it was not, unfortunately, a foregone conclusion that the attraction one might feel towards someone else would be reciprocated. He said nothing more and her curiosity as to whether or not he had ever found himself in such a situation remained unsatisfied. His reticence was reassuring, Alice persuaded herself, as it implied that he did not regard her as a disinterested 'older woman' to whom such confidences could be entrusted. But she suspected that if he *had* confided in her, then she would have chosen to regard such frankness as a confirmation of mutual trust and friendship.

Covertly observing him from her side of the table, Alice could see that Paul looked decidedly happy and she thought that she could also detect an underlying element of excitement in his mood. Appreciative as he was of good food, she was reluctant to believe that it might only be the sight of the cheese (which he was tackling with enthusiasm) that was responsible for his expression.

'The work on the flat's coming along nicely. The plasterer should have finished by tomorrow.'

Alice did her best to echo his pleasure. She had also contrived to sound sincere when some time earlier she had sympathised with him over the delay in getting a plasterer to even start the work.

Thank God,' he continued, 'it's at last beginning to look as though everything will be completed before I take off at the end of September.'

'You're going on holiday?'

'Well, yes and no.' Paul leaned forward and now there was no mistaking the excitement in his face.

'As a matter of fact, I will be combining business with pleasure. You see, I've had an idea simmering in my mind for ages and lately I've decided that if I don't get on and do something about it soon, it'll remain one of those dreams that are never fulfilled. Don't you find that it's the things left undone in one's life that fill one with regret rather than the things one has actually done – even the reprehensible things?' He didn't pause for a response but hurried on.

'What I really want to do is run an antique business somewhere in Provence. I'm going to hunt around for something suitable in Aix, or perhaps Arles,' he shrugged, 'Vauvenargues, maybe. Well, there are so many places I fancy in the Basses-Alpes region or the Bouches-du-Rhône. I'll scout around Avignon, too. The whole area is so beautiful that one is almost spoilt for choice. But I expect you know Provence?'

Alice shook her head.

'No? Well you must, you really must experience it for yourself. We must do something about that. The quality of the light, Alice, it's, well . . . indescribable! I don't think there's anywhere in the world where I would rather live.'

'You make me wish I was coming with you!'

'From a business point of view, too, I'm sure it's a sound

idea. Too much of the best English stuff in the trade has been going across the channel by the lorry load; I think it's high time to try to reverse that flow. I plan to build on the contacts I already have with French buyers, put that together with my contacts here and establish a two-way trade, so to speak.'

'But your shop here in Tern Bay – what's going to happen to that? You can't be in two places at the same time.' Oh no! she thought, as the awful possibility struck her that the refurbishment of his flat had been undertaken preparatory to selling both it and the business.

'Let me explain. What I hope to do is to keep the shop here in Tern Bay in addition to running a business in France. I want to have a foot in both camps. Commute, if you like! It'll mean having a really reliable assistant in both shops so that I'll feel free to shuttle between the two – do you see?'

Paul refilled his wine glass. If he hadn't been so absorbed in his plans, he would surely have noticed that her own was empty, thought Alice, giving her glass a little nudge in the vain hope of making him aware of his uncharacteristic oversight.

'As a matter of fact, I've already arranged for an old friend to run the shop here in my absence. He'll be starting just before I leave on my recce trip; that'll give him a chance to learn the ropes. Simon has a very sound knowledge of the trade – silver and porcelain, in particular. You'll like him, I'm sure.'

He paused to tear a cluster of grapes from the bunch flanking the cheese.

'I've also had tentative talks with a French chap whom I've dealt with in the past and I'm pretty sure he'd like to work for me in the Provence side of the business. His contacts could be valuable and he's very knowledgeable about

French provincial furniture. There's a growing interest in that over here – that's a line I want to develop.'

'You seem to have it all very well planned, I must say!'

Perhaps sensing an aggrieved tone in her voice, Paul placed his hand over Alice's which lay on the table tightly clenched round her crumpled napkin.

'You're one of the few people here that I've mentioned any of this to. You know how it is, I didn't want to talk about my plans until things were really under way. In any case, it's by no means all cut and dried yet. Unfortunately, there could be snags.'

'Difficulties in finding suitable premises?'

'No, not that. But I really oughtn't to bore you with my plans.' Paul released Alice's hand and started to fold his napkin, matching crease on crease with slow deliberation.

'Tell me. What is the problem?'

'Well, it's . . . Alice, I really would like to keep on the shop here in Tern Bay. For many reasons, as I expect you can guess. But, ultimately, that will depend on what I may have to fork out for the premises in France. You see, I had hoped that Simon might be able to put up some cash and buy himself a partnership in my present shop; but, as it turns out, he just can't raise that sort of money. He came a bit of a cropper recently over some investment that didn't work out as he had hoped. It's just one of those things. So, if it comes to the bit, I may very well be forced to sell out in order to set up in France.'

'What can I say, Paul, except that I do hope it doesn't come to that. If you left altogether it would be such a loss . . . well, to all of us.'

Alice's voice tailed off into a silence which Paul seemed content to leave unbroken. Surely, she thought, common social courtesy requires him to say something, dammit! She raised her eyes hoping for any little sign of regret that their relationship (friendship, or whatever he saw it as being) was in danger of not being granted time to develop any further.

Paul wasn't looking at her. Elbows resting on the table, he was rhythmically stroking one side of his face, right fore-finger lightly tracing a line from temple to mid-chin, slowly, repetitively.

'Finding the cash, that's always the rub. Still, it may work out O.K. No good worrying too much about it at this stage,' he added, concerned, at least, with offering comfort to himself.

'I'm going to make the coffee.' Alice rose abruptly.

At the door, hearing Paul start to clear the table, she turned and, her voice sharp, told him to leave everything, as she would attend to it later.

Paul joined her in the kitchen while she was still glumly waiting for the water to boil. 'Alice,' he said, his voice apologetic, 'I'm sorry if I've sprung my plans on you too suddenly – and at such boring length.'

'Goodness, you haven't been boring about it! Whatever gave you that idea? But it has surprised me a little that you gave me no hint before now of what was in your mind. There have been opportunities, I would have thought. But there it is. Just hand me the coffee jar, would you?'

'But, Alice,' he persisted, adopting a light teasing tone in response to her matter-of-fact one, 'even if I am forced to sell the shop here, you won't be getting rid of me altogether. You'll see, I'll be popping in to see you when I come back on business!'

Alice was measuring out the coffee. 'If you'd like a brandy with your coffee, just fetch one for yourself – the bottle's on the sideboard. I'll bring the coffee into the drawing room in a minute.

'Don't pour one for me,' she called after him.

When she carried the coffee tray into the drawing room, she found him comfortably seated, quite evidently enjoying his solitary drink and stroking the cat who had curled herself up on his lap and was contentedly purring with a noise like a simmering kettle. Perfidious animal, thought Alice.

She asked Paul not to bother to rise, but her request was terse and delivered a fraction of a second before he was able to show any intention of disturbing either himself or April.

Alice had looked forward to telling him about the cat, amusing him with a recital of her visit to the formidable Maud although carefully omitting from her account the more disturbing and personal aspects of the morning's encounter. But now she found herself satisfying his curiosity about this new addition to her household with the sparsest of information.

At last, breaking one of the uneasy silences which fell between them, Paul said, his voice quiet and sympathetic, 'Alice, I really had no idea that the prospect of my leaving Tern Bay would upset you so much. It just never occurred to me . . .'

'Upset? Good heavens, I'm not upset! A little annoyed, perhaps, that you didn't confide your plans before now. No doubt that is rather silly of me because, after all, there's no earthly reason why you should have done.'

'Exactly! But the fact remains that you do feel hurt. Please, I do apologise – what more can I say? But, in any case, it is by no means a foregone conclusion that I will have to relinquish entirely the shop in Tern Bay. The need for raising extra capital may not even arise. Let's not talk about it any more – what do you say, shall we call pax?'

'Why not?' Alice smiled and tried not to feel like a child whose petulant and unreasonable behaviour was being tactfully brushed aside.

For the remainder of the evening Paul entertained her

with an assiduousness which, in other circumstances, Alice would have found flattering.

When he had driven away and the cat, who had taken advantage of the opening of the front door to streak out into the night, had at last been persuaded to return, Alice was so exhausted that she felt unable to summon sufficient energy even to climb the stairs to bed.

She went to the dining room, took the brandy bottle from the sideboard and dropped into a chair at the uncleared table. I don't even like brandy, Alice thought, turning the bottle round and round in her hands. She'd only got it in for Paul. Egg-nog laced with brandy, raising Oliver's head from the pillow. Restorative brandy.

Disinclined to rise to fetch a clean glass, she poured herself a large drink into the one nearest to hand, which happened to be Paul's. Neither the dregs of the wine nor the kiss which might, or might not, have been left within (it had certainly not been otherwise bestowed) modified the immediate comfort bestowed by the brandy. That, she thought, looking with some surprise at the glass which she had drained so quickly, was downed purely for medicinal purposes and to such effect that she felt energetic enough to get up and refill her glass.

I handled things badly, she told herself, now sipping her drink in a more decorous and reflective manner and reasoning that as she did not like either the smell or the taste she was in no danger of being self-indulgent. How, she asked herself, turning the knife with cruel objectivity, how could I have been so gauche as to let him see how much the prospect of his leaving Tern Bay distresses me? But perhaps the truth is, she conceded, that I hadn't myself realised, until faced with the possibility of it ending, just how much his company has come to mean to me.

At least, she comforted herself, absentmindedly helping

herself to a grape, I didn't embarrass him by rushing in and offering him a loan to ensure that he wouldn't have to face parting with his Tern Bay shop. How squalid a half-demolished bunch of grapes looks, she thought, gazing with distaste at the detritus of the meal which she had so carefully prepared such a long, long time ago.

But if, on the other hand, I had immediately offered financial help, it might well have appeared as no more than the spontaneous and natural gesture of a friend. Well, for better or worse, the opportunity for that quick and unreflective response had come and gone. If I offer help the next time we meet, she thought, my offer will be seen as being made after consideration and, as such, will be liable to be interpreted as being born of self-interest. It would be too awful if he regarded it as an attempt on my part to make him feel beholden. And, of course, he would be right – wouldn't he? She rose and poured herself another drink with some hope of drowning that objective self-analysing voice.

With some idea that it was unwise to drink so much without eating, she resolutely ate the last of the grapes, flaccid and warm though they were, and turned her attention dutifully to the cheese and biscuits.

There is no aspect of life, however apparently privileged, that does not carry within it the seeds of its own peculiar disadvantage, she thought, dislodging a grape-pip from her teeth and recalling her happy and uncomplicated relationship with Oliver. Now she was called upon to pay the price, because it now seemed to her that during these long years of contented marriage her talent to handle relationships with men other than Oliver had simply atrophied from lack of use. Even her ability, whether instinctive or reasoned, to arrive at decisions had been eroded by the years, during which she had relied upon Oliver's help to resolve doubts.

It was not so much that she had relied upon him for advice upon which to act, but that he had always been ready to listen, and from the very recital of her problems had often sprung their solution.

Far from the passing of the years having matured me, brought me wisdom, they've emotionally stunted me, she thought dourly, forcing herself to finish the cheese which she had so lavishly and unthinkingly loaded on to a biscuit. Any youngster in her twenties would know exactly how to handle this situation, could resolve it standing on her head – or, more likely, lying on her back.

But what exactly is 'this situation'? Surely there must have been a time when she would have known, without having to give the matter any conscious thought at all, whether or not a man was sufficiently attracted to her for him to be reassured, rather than frightened off, by any sign on her part that her feelings were deeper than might have been immediately apparent?

It was an acknowledged fact that many people regressed with age to a state of second childhood. Surely then, before one reached that stage of regression one would first have to experience some sort of re-run of adolescence? That, thought Alice, amazed at her own percipience and finishing off her fourth, or it might have been her fifth, brandy, is exactly what is happening to me! The diagnosis brought no comfort.

When, for the second time that evening, Alice contemplated the stairs, the task of climbing them seemed no less daunting than before, although the reason for her difficulty in mounting them had changed. Half-way up she sat down, which seemed only sensible as the bannisters persistently eluded her grasp. A show of independence on her part might well persuade them to behave less tiresomely. The real question, she told herself, looping her arms round her knees, is whether, if I could be really confident of living my life happily on my own, I would still find myself so attracted to Paul. She closed her eyes the better to concentrate and then hastily opened them again, alarmed by the dizzying sensation of spinning into space which their closing had induced. The hallway below looked very far away and very dark, a featureless void waiting for her fall.

To hell with the bannisters, she decided, completing her progress to the landing on hands and knees.

A liberal splashing of cold water on her face sobered her sufficiently to feel dismayed at the sensation of comfort she experienced on finding April waiting for her on her bed.

Later, she awakened to a dreadful stillness and with a raging thirst. Moonlight, bleak and lifeless flooded the room. She fetched herself a glass of water from the bathroom, padding unsteadily down the corridor in bare feet, finding her way illuminated by the same blanched light. Why, she wondered, when she had returned to her bedroom and was gazing at the moon that stared at her through the uncurtained window, why is the moon considered romantic when, in fact, its stare is in reality so baleful? She closed the curtains, blotting out that lunatic glare and stumbled in the darkness to her bed.

She insinuated herself gingerly between the sheets, anxious not to disturb the cat who slept on, a warm circle of gently breathing life in the middle of the daunting width of her grandparents' bed.

Alice had left the back door ajar after letting April out; now there seemed no choice but to open it wider in response to the loud knock which reverberated in her head with the force of a wave breaking on rock.

It was Thelma, who stood on the doorstep looking excessively wholesome and wide awake.

Alice, clutching her dressing gown close, eyes screwed up

against the cruel strength of the early morning light, peered disbelievingly at her visitor.

'Thelma! I thought perhaps it might be the milkman . . .'

'Sorry to disappoint you, old thing. I say, you do look pretty rough!'

Alice opened the door wider as Thelma was pawing the scraper with her muddy wellington boots and clearly expected to be invited inside.

'Thought I'd best come round to the back as I'm a bit mucky – it's those damned geese; the mess they leave in the yard is beyond belief, great dollops! Never mind, we'll be shot of them by Christmas.' She broke off to stare at Alice. 'Heavens! What have you been up to?'

'Nothing. That's to say, well, it's only just after seven and I didn't sleep too well.'

Thelma plonked herself down by the kitchen table. 'Yes, I suppose it is a bit early to call, but I was on my way to look at a couple of field drains and as I was passing your door I thought I'd just pop in as there's something I want to ask you.'

Alice eased the kettle over the pile of unwashed pans in the sink. 'I'm going to make myself some coffee – fancy a cup?'

'Rather!' Thelma was taking in the uncharacteristic disorder of Alice's kitchen. 'Been having a bit of a party?'

'Not really. Just a friend to dinner.' Alice was guiltily aware that she still owed Thelma and Toby a meal.

'You've heard about Jonathan, I expect. Silly chump!'

'Yes. Very nasty.'

'Damned funny though!' Thelma, observing Alice's wince, broke off in mid-neigh and, scraping back her chair and rolling up the sleeves of her flannel shirt, attempted to elbow Alice away from the sink.

'Sorry,' said Alice, having rather tersely dissuaded her

from washing up the pans. 'I'm not at my best, first thing. What is it you wanted to ask me?'

'Actually, what I was wondering was whether I could put you down for a pup.'

Alice, mystified, waited for enlightenment while Thelma rootled in the tin of Bath Olivers which remained on the table from the previous evening.

'Binky – remember? She's due to whelp some time next month, poor old girl.'

'Can't you just drown them?' Alice, carefully placing the cups of coffee on the table and hoping that Thelma wouldn't notice how they rattled on their saucers, looked up to meet her disapproving frown.

'I suppose one could if one was that sort of person.' Thelma's voice was frosty. Clearly the disposal of geese was one thing, of puppies quite another. 'I happen to think it'd be heartless not to leave Binky with at least one. Just as well that I left her out in the car – I wouldn't like her to have heard you discussing her pups so callously.'

Alice raised her eyebrows, not certain whether Thelma was hoping to be taken seriously.

'No good putting on that supercilious expression, Alice. I'm perfectly certain that intelligent domesticated animals do know what human beings are thinking – I don't mean that they understand the words as such, but they sense what we're on about. Just imagine how you'd feel if you were pregnant and sensed that people were speculating about whether or not it wouldn't be best for your baby to be got rid of.'

Alice remembered (would she ever forget?) Samantha confiding in her that she and David had decided that, things being so unsettled between them, her pregnancy ought to be terminated. Flattered by being so unexpectedly taken into her daughter-in-law's confidence and eager, perhaps, to appear liberated and 'with-it', Alice had refrained from protest. When the courage to uphold her instinctive convictions had returned, it had been too late and her grandchild had already been sluiced away into the sewers of London. It was all very well for people to say that one should trust one's instincts but, in fact, everything in life conspired to distance one from instinct. But some people seemed to have retained a talent for deciding, without equivocation, just what ought to be done about anything and everything. Thelma, spraying crumbs of biscuit over the table as she laid down the law with such certainty, was just such a person, thought Alice with an irritation coloured by envy.

'But surely that's exactly what lots of people do nowadays – I mean, discuss whether or not their young should be allowed to live?'

'Oh, people! People are capable of all sorts of depravity,' said Thelma scornfully. 'But Binky's a bitch, a nice, decent little bitch. In any case, she ought to be left with at least one pup – for the milk, you see. I'm surprised at you Alice, really I am! Besides, I thought you'd be pleased to be given first refusal. Of course if you don't like dogs, then that's different.'

'But I *do* – at least, I don't actually dislike dogs . . . in general.'

'Well there you are then! Now's your chance to have one. Of course I can't guarantee what it'll *look* like. But I'd put my money on the sire being Polly Cornford's corgi and he's quite a good-looking little chap; nice nature too, as corgis go. Poor dog can't help the sort of owner he is inflicted with. It could be quite an interesting cross – dachshund and corgi. But if you're not interested in breeding, then it's not the looks that matter so much in a companion – it's the character, isn't it?'

Alice, finding herself in complete agreement, nodded.

'Well then, look at Binky! Loyal, loving, cheerful, never smelly – what more could one want? Perfect company for someone on her own like you, Alice. I really believe you could go a long way before you'd find a better bet as a companion than one of Binky's offspring. Ideally, I think you ought to have a dog in preference to a bitch – less trouble.' With a wave of her hand Thelma silenced Alice's attempt to interrupt.

'Oh I know that a dog can nip off after the odd bitch, but they do come back and no harm done. Personally, though, I prefer a bitch's nature, but there's no denying that their little peccadillos can have unfortunate repercussions.'

'Thelma! If you'd just allow me to get a word in! I'm sure you're right; a pet would be a good idea, but the thing is, I already have one.'

'You have? Why didn't you tell me before?'

'Because I've only just acquired her – look, there she is!' said Alice, nodding her head in the direction of the open door where April, perfectly on cue, stood silhouetted against the light as she paused to stare warily at the seated visitor before she strolled past, with a quickly assumed air of indifference, on her way upstairs to the bed which would not yet have lost its welcoming warmth.

'But that's your aunt's cat – I thought Nancy had taken her with her.'

Alice related how April had returned to Fernhurst and how, subsequently, the odious Maud had been only too pleased to allow Alice to keep her. 'So you see,' Alice concluded, 'I do have a pet now and April, who does have prior rights to living here, seems to be the sort of cat who would hate dogs so it's out of the question for me to even consider taking one of Binky's pups. It wouldn't be fair to either of them.'

'You're probably right. Damn!' Thelma rose. 'I'll be off

then.' She gave Alice another searching look. 'You're sure everything's O.K.?'

Alice, after almost imperceptible hesitation, nodded.

'Yes, of course! I must just remember to take more water with it next time. One gets out of practice – for so many things, I suppose.'

Binky was sitting abjectly in the passenger seat of Thelma's muddy Land Rover, her moist eyes reproachful. Alice congratulated herself that she had escaped having an animal of comparable lugubrious mien foisted upon her.

Thelma let in the clutch and poked her head out of the window for a last word. 'You ought to tell Miss Vine about the cat – she got her for your aunt after old Calico died; she'll be jolly chuffed to know that she came back.' She bent down and lifted something from the floor. 'I brought this for you – it's our own, none of that pasteurised muck.'

Alice took the carton of cream which Thelma thrust at her and, as though it were indeed as hot as coals of fire, held it stiffly at arm's length as she returned to the kitchen. She was relieved to shut the refrigerator door behind it; the very thought of the carton's rich thick contents sent ripples of nausea coursing through her.

There was relief too, that a dangerous corner had been successfully turned when, for a split second, she had been tempted to pour out to Thelma her muddled emotions about Paul. They're keeping an eye on me, the Old Girls, she thought, not sure whether she found the thought comforting or alarming.

Her legs weak at the recollection of how near she had come to indiscretion, Alice sat down – but not for long. Spurred on by the knowledge of the unwashed dishes in the sink, the uncleared table in the dining room and the cups rimmed with cold coffee still on the tray in the drawing room, she drove herself to the task of tidying up.

Frowning with distaste as her fingers cleared from the sink the clammy debris left in the wake of the washing up, she told herself that perhaps she ought to do something about engaging some domestic help. The problem was that if she did so, then she would be left with more time to fill. She could sew lampshades; improve her mind by enrolling in one of the classes so enthusiastically attended by Clare and Desmond; offer her services as one of the vicar's flower-arranging ladies and learn how to stick wires up inoffensive larkspur; join one of Polly Cornford's charitable committees and organise knit-ins for old age pensioners; bottle fruit and bake Victoria sponges for the Conservative Women's Bring and Buy. There were so many ways in which one could occupy oneself in order that the sum total of their littleness could furnish the illusion that one's life was not without purpose and fulfillment.

'For goodness sake, grow up!' she told herself, giving the dishcloth a vicious wring before flinging it from her and not permitting herself to wonder just what the injunction really meant.

Later, bathed, dressed, all traces of the previous evening's dinner cleared away and aspirins and bismuth having had time to take their effect, she felt, if not exactly spry, considerably more composed.

Alice, however, had never been able to rid herself of the notion that somewhere there sat a supreme all-seeing, all-knowing Judge whose pleasure it was to award good or bad conduct marks as appropriate. If the black mark undoubtedly earned by her over-indulgence with the brandy were to be cancelled out, then she must undertake some act of penance (her hangover – being involuntary – didn't really count). She could, she decided, pay a visit to Miss Vine; that ought to be worth a couple of good conduct marks.

*

Miss Vine, a hank of raffia draped round her neck like some outlandish boa, was busy staking her herbaceous-border plants and seemed genuinely pleased, if a little surprised, to receive a visit from Alice, who normally only appeared when summoned on some pretext or other.

Alice meekly complied as she was ordered to 'hand me that' or 'hold this' as Miss Vine, grunting a little and wielding a croquet mallet with no mean skill, drove home the support canes.

'That should do nicely,' she said, standing back to admire the last clump of Michaelmas daisies which she had imprisoned in a girdle of raffia. 'I'm a great believer in getting everything ship-shape before the autumn gales arrive.'

'But we're only half-way through August,' protested Alice.

'Exactly – no time at all until autumn. And then, when it is finally upon us,' Miss Vine bent a little stiffly to dragoon a wayward stem into confinement, 'all one can usefully do is batten down and accept the inevitability of the winter that lies ahead.'

Alice wished she could be sure that Miss Vine was discussing only the seasons of the year. She was instructed to load the wheelbarrow with the surplus canes and the other paraphernalia and return all to the garden shed while Miss Vine arranged suitable refreshment.

Miss Vine brought from the kitchen glasses and a jug of home-made lemon barley-water whose viscous surface supported a handful of leaves hastily plucked from the bed of mint which sprawled at the end of the vegetable patch. The concoction, too thick, deficient in sugar but too liberally endowed with lemon juice and unpleasantly tepid, was just as Alice remembered it when it had been an unwelcome feature of the refreshments served when Beech Park was entertaining a visiting team. Why on earth, Alice asked herself, chewing on a leathery leaf, should the reappearance of this awful brew fill me with a sudden compassion for its creator?

Although Alice was now more than a little bored by her own recital of the circumstances of the cat's return to Fernhurst, Miss Vine was gratifyingly interested in the story. Alice repaid the compliment by simulating a comparable interest in Miss Vine's account of how she had obtained April for Sophie by way of an appeal in the Old Beechonians' magazine.

'Now, about my little mag . . .' Miss Vine leaned forward and fixed Alice with a stare which was impossible to evade without giving the impression of being rather shifty. 'I know you've never been one of the subscribers, dear, but perhaps I could persuade you to make a small contribution. I don't mean in a financial sense,' she added, as Alice began to open the handbag on her lap. 'Of course an annual sub would not go amiss – the venture is non-profit-making, naturally, but expenses do have a way of rising these days. But what I really have in mind is a little article from you on the subject of coming to terms with living on one's own – the sort of thing that would be of help to many other Old Beechonians facing similar sad circumstances. I am making the assumption, wrongly perhaps, that you have resigned yourself to that situation. Now, Alice dear, what about it?' Miss Vine's eyes were shrewd, alert.

Alice, who had opened her mouth to decline, was left with it momentarily agape while Miss Vine rushed on. 'No, no, don't turn down the proposition immediately; think about it and let me know when you're ready. Looking at things squarely, getting your thoughts ordered on paper, could be very therapeutic, y'know.'

'No doubt.' Alice's tone was dry.

She contrived to change the subject by confiding the information that Nancy would be paying a visit to her sister in Tern Bay and that she proposed to invite her to Fernhurst during her stay.

'My word! First yourself, then April and now Nancy – all coming back to Fernhurst,' said Miss Vine. She added, reflectively, 'Like so many chickens coming home to roost!'

Alice heard herself asking, abruptly, 'How were things with Aunt Sophie – at the end?'

'I think that is one of the things you must ask Nancy.'

'But surely – well, I'd assumed that you were such close friends, you and Aunt Sophie . . .'

'Oh we were. Certainly at one time, very close. But life goes on and things change . . . although what has been leaves its reverberations, as it were. I believe that as a friend I did all that it was in my power to do for Sophie, but that was not as much as I would have liked. The circumstances were rather odd, y'know. Sophie had suffered a series of strokes, but no doubt you are aware of that.' Miss Vine smiled a tight little smile. 'Nancy became very possessive. I was rather fobbed off, one might say. Poor dear Sophie! But I did what I could, as, no doubt, did Nancy . . . in her own way.' Miss Vine, her thin lips set in an uncompromising tight line, fell silent.

Well, if she wants to play at being enigmatic, thought Alice, I'm certainly not going to give her the satisfaction of knowing how much I resent being kept in the dark. In any case she'll probably only tell me again that I must ask Nancy – and that is just what I shall do. Looking away from Miss Vine, her downward glance fell on her open bag. She took from it the carton of cream, a little crushed now, a crusted trickle clinging to its side.

'I brought you this.'

'How very kind!' Miss Vine took the gift with less than enthusiasm. 'Funnily enough, Thelma brought me some yesterday – how my Old Girls spoil me! But the real purpose of Thelma's visit was to try to talk me into taking one of the puppies that beastly bitch of hers is about to produce. She seems to think that my party had some bearing on Binky's predicament. My dear, I told her that if hosts were to be held responsible for every *mésalliance* resulting from their parties, then no one would have the courage to entertain at all.

'But,' she added, 'I'm not at all sure that you wouldn't be better to keep this for yourself, Alice. You do look a little peaky. Doing too much, are you – or is it a case of too little?'

'Neither, as far as I'm aware.' Alice snapped her bag shut.

'Please, dear, no need to take offence. Now I think I'd better put this in the fridge straight away; always such a pity when things turn sour from neglect.'

She placed her own and Alice's empty glass on the tray alongside the cream. 'I've always placed great faith in the restorative powers of my lemon barley and I do believe that you're already looking the better for it!' Miss Vine smiled approvingly at Alice whose colour had indeed heightened.

'I suppose you've heard,' said Miss Vine as they sauntered together in seeming amity towards the cottage, 'that Tom is no longer *persona grata* with the Cornford woman? I did hope that now that he is back again, and so unexpectedly early, he might lend a hand in my garden. But I rather suspect that he's found other fish to fry, temporarily at any rate.'

'Why don't you put an ad in the paper?'

'Oh no, I don't think I would fancy strangers about the place. "Better the devil you know" and all that . . .' Resting her hand against the trunk of an apple tree, Miss Vine suddenly declaimed:

'From his brimstone bed at break of day
A-walking the Devil is gone,
To visit his snug little farm the earth,
And see how his stock goes on.'

She paused, frowning. 'Now then, just how does it go on?
Ah yes –

His jacket was red and his breeches were blue,
And there was a hole where the tail came through.

Coleridge makes him sound rather a vulgar, jolly sort of
chap, and so very conspicuous, don't you think? But I think
of the Devil as shadowy and sly, crouching unseen in the
middle of the confusion he loves to create and given to
working in mysterious ways – a trick he probably picked up
in heaven before he was cast out.'

Miss Vine slipped her arm through Alice's and accompanied her to the gate. 'As a matter of fact,' she said, 'I have
solved the problem of help in the garden. Apparently Clare's
Desmond has taken to what I believe is called "the health
kick"; what ghastly expressions are coined nowadays! Apart
from eating lentils and bean shoots it involves a lot of exercise, jogging and so forth. Well, I rang Clare and suggested
that a spot of autumn digging would be much more produc-
tive than aimless jogging so she promised to send him along
at the weekend. It was Barbara who told me about
Desmond's latest fad. Did I mention that I popped in on her
the other day? I wanted to enquire about poor Jonathan and
to give her a bottle of my lemon barley to take along to the
hospital. I got the impression that she hadn't been expecting
any callers . . . I took her by surprise, one might say!'

Miss Vine closed the gate behind Alice. 'Now dear, be
sure to let me know how Nancy's visit goes. I enjoyed our

little talk, I really don't know how I'd manage to get along without my girls around me. They make me feel that being a very old spinster is not so terrible after all.' Alice glanced sharply at Miss Vine, but the smile of her old headmistress seemed blandly innocent.

8

~

This, Alice reflected, would be the first occasion on which Nancy had been entertained in Fernhurst, and had been offered food and drink that was not of her own preparation. Alice had spared no pains, and, indeed, taken pleasure in arranging things as perfectly as she was able in readiness for Nancy's visit. She was grateful for the opportunity of expressing in so practical a fashion her gratitude to Nancy for the years of devoted service she had rendered.

She put the finishing touches to the tea-tray which stood on the kitchen table ready to be carried to the drawing room at the appropriate time. The cloth and matching linen napkins had been embroidered by Sophie, the silver tea-service had been polished with as much meticulous care as Nancy had ever lavished upon it. Perhaps, Alice thought, it did have a certain spinsterish look about it; she whisked away the little muslin square, weighted with beads at each corner, with which she had covered the cream jug.

In the dim coolness of the larder, primly wrapped in cling film, finely cut sandwiches, miniature chocolate éclairs and a coffee and walnut cake of particular excellence awaited arrangement on the tiered cake stand. It had been a small triumph, locating that ancient cake stand. As she had unwrapped it from its blue tissue paper shroud, Alice had permitted herself a moment of unashamedly sentimental reflection. She recalled how thin slices of brown bread and butter used to fill the lowest tier, scones would be placed on the second and fruit cake and cream pastries would have pride of place on the topmost plate. Under the critical eye of her grandmother she had never dared violate the rule that one had to start at the bottom and decorously work one's way up to the rich delights of the top tier. It was, Aunt Sophie had explained, like a little parable about life. But wasn't there a danger, Alice had once anxiously inquired, that one might lose one's appetite by the time one had worked one's way up to the creamy rewards of the final tier? Grandmother had supplied the answer to that, rather snappishly as Alice recalled, by pointing out that that, too, constituted one of the unavoidable hazards of life, but one unlikely as yet to threaten Alice – blessed as she was with the healthy appetite of a child.

Well, thought Alice, her appetite had certainly not as yet deserted her for the little cream buns which life had placed in her way over the last few weeks. She had continued to see Paul, albeit not as frequently as during the period when his domestic life had been thrown into turmoil by the builders; but that had, after all, been an exceptional period. He had entertained her twice to dinner in his refurbished flat. She had brought him, as a house-warming present, a Rosenthal fruit service from her grandfather's collection. Paul had greatly admired the plates when he had seen them in use at Fernhurst. He had also assured her that they were the genuine article, which had slightly surprised Alice to whom it had not occurred that they might not be. He had rewarded her for her gift (after the usual 'you really oughtn't to have' protestations) with a kiss. A chaste, devoted-nephew type of kiss bestowed in the region of her cheekbone; but a kiss, for all that.

On the second occasion she had met Simon who had, as promised, moved in 'to learn the ropes'. A civil and pleasant enough man, Alice conceded, a trifle grudgingly. She acknowledged that she might have liked him more if she had not been a trifle jealous of him. She envied him the long friendship which he and Paul had enjoyed; it made her feel rather an outsider. But if Simon had been amused or surprised at Paul's friendship with a woman who was so much older than him, then he had not given the slightest indication of it. Alice succeeded in dismissing the disturbing thought that Simon's lack of critical interest might indicate that he considered the friendship to be of little consequence.

Paul had decided to leave Simon in sole charge of the shop for a day and had suggested that he and Alice go up to London together. It was all very correct but, nevertheless, highly enjoyable. They had looked in at Sotheby's, gone to a concert and enjoyed an excellent dinner.

At no time had Paul made any further mention of his plans; that did not surprise Alice when she remembered how she had reacted when he had first broached the subject during that unhappy little dinner at Fernhurst which she had done her best to forget.

But it was now becoming increasingly difficult for her to avoid facing the fact that things were about to change. Paul's plans were already underway. At the moment the shop was closed; he was driving around the country introducing Simon to trade connections. Alice knew that shortly after their return, Paul would be leaving for France. He'd come and see her before he left, he had said. Perhaps, she thought, it would be a good ploy for me not to be here, waiting, when he returns. She could go up to London for a couple of days: see old friends, do some shopping. A note could be put through the letterbox at the shop, a casual 'sorry to have missed you, hope you have a good trip' sort of message. Or would that be too childish, too transparent a declaration that she was not to be taken for granted? The trouble is, I'm not sure just how I wish to be taken – if at all.

If Nancy felt distress at returning as a visitor to the house which had been her home for over fifty years, then she did not betray it. She had paused in the doorway of the drawing room and expressed pleasure, but no surprise, at finding the room virtually unchanged. There was a certain dignity about her, an air of quiet, brave resolve. She looks, Alice thought, rather like a woman in a dentist's waiting-room who has steeled herself to endure a painful ordeal but who is determined, from motives of self-respect or out of regard for the sensibilities of the other waiting patients, to preserve an outward appearance of calm.

She sat opposite Alice, her back to the light; her long thin feet in their highly polished black Oxfords arranged neatly side by side; her hands, lightly cupped one within the other, rested upon her lap. It would not be possible to say that Nancy looked either older or younger than her years; she was one of those women who struck one as being of indeterminate age and, in Alice's eyes, looked much as she had done twenty or even thirty years ago. She was, perhaps, a trifle thinner and her wiry frame had acquired a bird-boned fragility. Her well-pressed navy linen suit of timeless cut had the appearance of a lovingly cherished outfit which, in Alice's imagination, spent the greater part of its existence swathed in tissue paper and carefully hung on a padded hanger. Alice could detect a slightly darker tone in the bottom two inches of the hem of the skirt. There was a poignancy about that subtle colour differentiation which caused Alice to hastily shift her gaze.

A little silence gathered and congealed. The initial exclamations of mutual pleasure occasioned by the reunion, the polite exchange of superficial information, had run their course and they were both now composing themselves for confidences of a weightier order.

'Nancy,' Alice began, hesitantly, 'I know how devoted you were to my aunt and I don't want to cause you distress but now that some time has passed since her death I wonder if perhaps you could explain for me some things which have been puzzling me. I know that it's my own fault that I have to ask – I ought to have made more effort to come to see her, to see for myself how things were for her at the end. It was very wrong of me, and I do reproach myself.'

'You must try not to feel like that, you have nothing to blame yourself for! After all, you had your family obligations; we both knew and understood that.'

'But quite apart from my duty towards Aunt Sophie, you were entitled to receive more support from me. Oh, Nancy, what can I say?'

'Looking back, I think that I was in the wrong not to have let you know exactly how things were going, but I knew that Mr Willoughby was very ill and I didn't want to add to your anxieties. Besides, I didn't really think that you, or anybody else for that matter, could do much that would help.' Nancy paused, her eyes looking beyond Alice. 'And as for me being entitled to support, do you know I don't think that I've ever thought in terms of "entitlement".' The remark held no undertone of reproof, rather it was made as though Nancy were quite objectively considering such an attitude to life.

'Nancy, there's Aunt Sophie's room! I just don't understand why she spent the end of her days in such . . . well, privation. Why, Nancy, why?'

'It was what she wanted. Miss Sophie had changed a great deal, and I don't mean only as a result of her last stroke. No, it had started before that – the change in her. At first I thought she'd return to being her old self, given time. But it didn't work out that way. Things weren't easy.'

'But what sort of a change was it, and when did it start? I mean, I saw her when I came down for Grandma's funeral and she seemed her usual self then. Very tired, of course, and sad – but that wasn't surprising.'

'It was soon after your grandmother's death that things started to change. Of course she was very tired – we both were; the old lady's illness had taken a toll, you could see that. The sparkle seemed to go out of your aunt. She'd always been so cheery and full of fun.'

Alice nodded, remembering.

'She took to lying in bed till late in the morning – and that wasn't like her at all. She wouldn't be reading or listening to her radio either; she'd just lie there, not saying anything, not doing anything. She wouldn't hear of me calling in the doctor; said there was nothing to be gained from it. But I did get her a tonic from Boots and she did take that, but it didn't seem to make any difference. I wanted her to try some stuff that I saw in the health food shop, some sort of root that the girl there laid great store by, but she said it would be just a waste of money – it was about then that she began to get a bit odd about spending money. She wouldn't move back to her own nice bedroom, either. She'd taken to sleeping in that slip of a room next to your grandmother's when she was nursing the old lady, and there she made up her mind to stay. Wouldn't budge, for all that I tried to persuade her.'

Alice interrupted. 'I think I can understand her not wanting to bother to move while she was feeling so exhausted, but why wouldn't she have it made, well, a bit comfier?'

'But that was another funny thing. She deliberately stripped it of everything but the barest essentials. Wouldn't even hear of me putting in a vase of flowers to cheer it up a bit – and you know how she loved flowers. Always arranged them so beautifully. You've got her touch . . .' Nancy leaned forward and touched one of the late damask roses in the bowl on the table that stood between them. 'Always loved that colour, Miss Sophie did.'

'She was obviously in some state of deep depression, poor dear Sophie!'

Nancy nodded. 'It'll pass, I told myself, when she's had a bit of a rest. I did my best to jolly her up; I tried to act as though I didn't notice that there was something terribly wrong. I'd suggest little outings that we could make: perhaps take the car down to the sea and have a bathe and a picnic – you know the sort of thing. But she wouldn't have any of it. Then I'd try talking about all the things we could do together now that we weren't tied to nursing her mother; well, that sounds a bit callous, but I put it sort of tactfully. Once you're feeling yourself again, properly rested, you could have a little party for all your old friends, I'd say. Come to think of it, there weren't so many of her old friends left really. But there was still that Miss Vine, of course.'

After a pause, Nancy continued. 'She'd got out of touch with people, you see, what with one thing and another and her mother never bearing to have her out of her sight during those last years. All that could change now, I said, though perhaps not in so many words, if you know what I mean.'

'But she didn't seem interested?'

Nancy shook her head. 'At first she'd just listen without saying anything and then, one day, she rounded on me – quite fierce, really. "Do stop twittering, Nancy," was what she said and then suddenly she was shouting at me, saying that everything had come too late and that her whole life had been a waste, a bad joke, she said. At first I was quite glad to see her roused – even being angry was better than just that closed-up sort of sad silence. They always say that convalescents get irritable, don't they? "Nonsense," I told her, "you've years ahead of you yet, you've got your health and you've got the money to enjoy yourself too. You can have a really nice time with only yourself to think about for a change!" But that only set her off worse than ever. "I have nothing," was what she said, and then, "and I'm worth nothing to anybody, certainly not to myself." And then suddenly she stopped raging and started to cry. That wasn't like her, either. It really upset me, that did, more than her shouting. I don't think I'd ever seen your aunt cry before, not in that wild despairing sort of way. She'd told me once that her days of weeping had come and gone long ago.'

'What was it that had made her cry – so long ago, I mean?' Alice's voice was soft, she felt as wary as if she were stalking a butterfly.

'Things that had gone all wrong for her when she'd been just a girl. It's all so much water under the bridge now.' Nancy sounded uncomfortable.

'It must have been something that I never heard about.'

'Well, it all happened before you were born, even before I came to work here. I expect that is how you never knew about it. Not,' added Nancy firmly, 'that there was any reason for you to know.'

A little stung, Alice said with equal firmness. 'But if I'm to understand what brought about Sophie's dreadful despair, perhaps I ought to know about it now, Nancy. After all, as you say, it was all a very long time ago so surely confiding whatever it was now can't do anyone any harm. But it

might have a bearing on things. How can I know, if you
don't tell me? Surely you're as concerned as I am to get to
the bottom of what caused poor Aunt Sophie to behave in
such an odd way. I know it's too late to do anything about
it now, but I'd like at least to try to *understand*.'

Nancy was silent for a moment, fiddling with the little
seed-pearl brooch that fastened the neck of her blouse.

'Yes, perhaps you're right. I did think it had a bearing,
but it wasn't anything that could be altered or put right.
Over the years we became very close, your aunt and
myself. We were more like old friends really than employer
and servant, you know? Sometimes we'd talk together
about the past, sharing the bits of our lives that we hadn't
lived together. There we were, two women together, and
her a bit lonely at times.' Nancy hesitated. 'I've never
repeated anything she told me about herself, but perhaps
there's no harm in it now and with her being your aunt,
it's not like spreading it outside the family, is it?'

Alice murmured reassurance.

'The thing was, you see, that when Miss Sophie was a
girl, her great friend was Miss Vine – Cornelia, your aunt
called her, of course. Close as close they were – like sisters
I should think. They were both at the same boarding
school and with Cornelia's parents being abroad – India, I
think it was – she usually spent the school holidays here
with Miss Sophie and her sister – your mother, that is. I
got the impression that your mother didn't like Cornelia;
jealous of sharing Miss Sophie with her, I suppose. It
seems that after a time your grandparents also took against
Cornelia. Then the headmistress (my, how Miss Sophie
still seemed to hate her, even after so long!), she wrote and
suggested to your grandparents that it might be better if
they didn't invite Cornelia to stay with them for every
holiday as she didn't believe in encouraging such intense

friendships between her girls. Sounds daft to me, but there it was! So what with that and them having taken a dislike to Cornelia themselves and your mother being a bit jealous too, it seems that your grandparents did their best to discourage the friendship. But, of course, they couldn't prevent them seeing each other altogether – they still went to the same school, after all. I expect the disapproval made them all the closer, really; you know how it is with young people. Well, Miss Sophie knew that Cornelia was set on going to the University, so she put her back into her schoolwork so that she could go with her. But when the time came, your grandfather wouldn't hear of her going. In those days, you know, however clever you were, if your parents couldn't or wouldn't pay the fees you just couldn't get to university. So that was that. Miss Sophie said that at the time she felt it was the end of the world. She'd so set her heart on it and had worked so hard to get accepted.'

'Poor Aunt Sophie – oh, I never knew!'

'Well, your grandparents thought it would all just blow over. Off Cornelia went to the University and they weren't sorry to see the pair of them parted, as they thought. But they wrote to each other every day. Cornelia Vine sent her letters to Miss Sophie by way of a friend in the village so that your grandparents wouldn't know. Fancy Miss Sophie doing something like that! They hatched a plan, you see. Cornelia had set her heart on running a school of her own once she'd finished her education and Miss Sophie would be her partner and they'd be together for always. Miss Sophie was to try and talk her father into putting up some of the money, a sort of dowry for a career instead of for a marriage, Miss Sophie said.

'Anyway. Then that Mr Dunster, who had just inherited Combe Farm from his father, started setting his cap at

Miss Sophie. But she wouldn't have any of it. I won't repeat what she called him; she could be quite salty, your aunt! Your grandparents were all for the match but they couldn't make any headway with her. They were anxious to get her settled because they knew that Cornelia was by then nearly finished at the University and she'd soon be back on the scene. They'd heard that she was already on the look-out for some place in this area where she could start a school. Her father had died – Miss Cornelia's, that is – and her mother married again out there abroad but Cornelia had inherited a bit of cash and she'd be able to use that to at least make a start. So there they were, your grandparents, doing their best to make Miss Sophie's life a misery: cajoling, bullying, and her with not a penny of her own to get away from all the rows and storms. Not that your grandmother stormed, that wasn't her way. No, I reckon she'd just have refused to discuss it after saying what she wanted. She'd have gone silent and icy and that can be worse than shouting.'

Seeing the distress in Alice's face, Nancy went on hastily. 'Now, don't you go getting things wrong! When your aunt told me all this, she made a sort of story out of it, laughing about it as though it had all happened to someone else. She was always so sweet and contented like, as if she had put it all away long ago. She was a bit like someone looking at old photos and having a bit of a laugh at how funny the hats look when you see them so long afterwards and you can't imagine however you came to be wearing them! You know? She even laughed when she told me about the time she went for a swim and made up her mind to go on swimming further and further out until she'd wear herself out and drown. But she saw she was swimming into a shoal of jellyfish – and you know how frightened she was of jellyfish! – and she turned back for the shore in a great panic. How absurd she'd been, she said, joking about it to me.'

'Did her parents know what she'd tried to do?'

'Oh, I don't expect so. Anyway, she didn't say. But they must have begun to see that they couldn't wear her down with bullying because when she asked your grandfather if she could get away for a bit to think things over, he gave in and agreed. She said that she might feel more inclined to bury herself in marriage if she had had a taste of freedom and independence first. They talked it over, your grandparents. It seems that your grandmother had an old friend who ran a sort of little school in Paris for English girls who'd just finished ordinary school. Languages and art and how to cook fancy things – that sort of place. So it was agreed that Miss Sophie could go there for a while, and off she went. Of course later they were furious because by the time she came home again George Dunster had got himself engaged to someone else. I remember that his little girl used to come here to play with you, you know who I mean? Thelma, that was her name.'

Alice nodded. Nancy, she could see, was well into her stride by now, recounting the tale almost as though it had ceased to have any personal relevance to the Sophie they had both known.

'Well, back home again and with Romeo out of the way, Miss Sophie did all she could to persuade your grandfather to put some money into Cornelia's projected school and to allow her to make a career there and to accept that marriage didn't appeal to her at all. She felt qualified to teach French by then, even although she hadn't got to university. But still he wouldn't budge. So she never did get what she'd set her heart on.

'Cornelia managed to raise the rest of the cash she needed and she started up Beech Park without Miss Sophie. Of course her parents couldn't prevent Miss Sophie and Cornelia seeing one another – what with her being just up at Beech Park – but, of course, things changed between them. What with Miss Vine having her career and being so busy and having a whole lot of new friends round her, she didn't have much time over for Miss Sophie. I expect Miss Vine felt that Miss Sophie hadn't been determined enough, but then she's a hard one, that Miss Vine. Always out for number one, she'd have been! But Miss Sophie was not one to put herself before others, not when it came to the bit. When your grandfather died he left everything to your grandmother, so Miss Sophie still hadn't a penny to her name. But even if she had, I don't think she would have felt able to desert her mother who had been left alone except for Miss Sophie; your own mother married and away by then, of course. So Miss Sophie just put all her dreams behind her and settled down to life with her mother.

'At least, she thought she'd put it all behind her and for years perhaps she had; but I think that at the end of the day and with your grandmother gone, bitterness set in and she started brooding over it. Well, it's only natural; as you get older you start wondering about what you've done with the years that are gone, don't you? I don't think she'd have been able to laugh about it all if she'd talked to me about the past after your grandmother's death. But she never did come over any of it again during those last months. I did wonder sometimes if she wanted to punish herself for having given up, for not having stood up for herself. Perhaps she was getting at her father, too, sort of showing him that, now that she was able to, she didn't want to touch his money. But I'm only guessing because I wasn't able to talk about things like that with her after your grandmother's death; she'd become different, you see – sort of distant, I'd lost touch with her.'

'Oh Nancy – I'd no idea about any of this.'

'It got worse,' said Nancy, driven now, it seemed, to leave nothing undisclosed. 'She got this bee in her bonnet that she didn't have any money at all! It went from her not wanting to touch the money to her not believing there was any there. I can't tell you how hard it was to squeeze a penny out of her for the barest essentials. I—' Nancy broke off in mid-sentence. There was a muffled, gentle padding on the door. 'That must be April!' she cried, 'I'd know that noise anywhere – she never puts her claws out when she wants a door opened, doesn't scratch it but just sort of thumps it.'

Alice rose and opened the door and April rushed past her with her long-legged rocking-horse canter and leapt on to Nancy's lap where she purred and arched her back and butted her head against Nancy's eager hands.

'Fancy her remembering me!' Nancy's eyes were bright with pleasure and a hint of something else. Alice, standing by the door and guiltily aware of a stab of jealousy, suggested she'd put on the kettle for their tea. Nancy insisted on following her and, with a practised movement, hitched the cat up on to her breast and shoulder.

Once in the kitchen, April leapt lightly on to the dresser where she settled herself comfortably, casting a look of smug defiance in Alice's direction.

'Oh the darling! She always loved to sit there and watch everything going on. The little rascal!' said Nancy indulgently, her voice gentle and sweet.

It was just the tone of voice in which Alice herself had so often been addressed in this very kitchen. On her way to the larder, Alice stopped in her tracks and, turning, impulsively threw her arms round Nancy.

Nancy, a little startled perhaps, patted Alice's back. Alice almost expected to hear the familiar words of comfort,

'There, there now, don't take on so – it'll soon be better.'

Releasing Nancy and feeling a little foolish, she said, 'It's just that . . . well, having you back and here in your own kitchen . . . Oh, Nancy, it's lovely, almost like old times.'

Nancy had seated herself at the table. 'Why don't we just have our tea here – like old times, as you said!'

A memory hung between them of shared cups of tea (Alice's milky and sweet), buns fresh from the oven and Nancy telling one of her stories to while away Alice's time until 'tea proper' with the grown-ups in the drawing room. Nice stories with happy endings to lighten an endless rainy afternoon.

Nancy praised everything: the sandwiches (she shared a crab-meat one with April, 'just a special little treat'), Alice's home-made éclairs and, of course, the cake. They recalled the day when, for the first time, Alice had made a batch of scones as a surprise for Sophie and they had turned out so leaden that Nancy had tactfully assisted her in eating them all up so that her failure would remain a secret between them. To have simply thrown them away would have been unthinkable, a case of flying in the face of Providence as Nancy would have put it, 'waste not, want not' having been one of her favourite axioms.

The initial shyness between them dissipated, Alice felt she might now safely broach the matter of her aunt's will.

'If my aunt really did come to believe that she had no money, was that the reason for her failing to make any provision for you in her will?' she asked, but with a reluctance that surprised her, considering how determined she'd felt to learn all that she could to explain Sophie's strange action. Now, with the explanation within sight, an instinct warned her that, in the end, she might learn more than she would wish.

Nancy shook her head. 'No, it wasn't that. She had a sound reason which I quite understood.'

'Well, *I* certainly don't understand! When I discovered that you weren't mentioned I was shocked – and very angry on your behalf. It's something that I intend to put right.'

'Perhaps if you knew the whole story, you'd feel differently.'

'Tell me.' Alice's voice was soft, almost inaudible. She sensed the thinness of the ice, could almost see the dead branches, the dark still weeds below.

Nancy was at first hesitant but then, as before, as her narrative took hold over her, her story flowed freely enough.

'It did all start with her not wanting to spend any money. She'd give me a cheque to get cash from the bank for day to day expenses, food and so forth. If I'd taken my wages out of it then there wouldn't have been enough to get by on. But I managed, one way or another.'

Nancy, her eyes intent on her task, was plucking April's hairs from her jacket; ginger, white, tan, conspicuous against the navy. 'She'd insisted that the central heating had to be turned off. I kept her room warm with a coal fire; she allowed that.' Rolling the fur into a little ball between her fingers, Nancy paused briefly. Alice had a vision of her carrying scuttles of coal up the stairs, the chill of the rest of the house striking through her.

'But it was when the bills came in that things got really difficult. "I'm not paying that!" she said when she saw the coal bill, the electricity bill. I told her we'd be cut off. She said there was nothing wrong with candles and if I put another couple of hot-water bottles in her bed then she could do without the fire; no good asking her how I was to boil the water with no electricity and no fuel for the Aga. She just refused to discuss it. In the end I paid the coal bill out of my Post Office Savings. I had to – else they wouldn't deliver any more.' Nancy sounded apologetic.

'Then the final notice came for the electricity. I didn't know where to turn. For one thing, I wasn't really sure if she had the money or not. You hear things about people losing everything with a bad investment. I remember my dad being left owed a lot of money by an old gentleman who'd suddenly lost everything, rubber shares I think it was. That was before the war, there used to be quite a lot of that sort of thing. Suddenly, everything gone, just like that. The way I saw it was that if I went to Miss Sophie's solicitor or to the bank and it turned out that the money side was all right, then they'd begin to wonder if she was quite right in the head. Well, they would, wouldn't they? Between them, they might think it best to have her put away somewhere, that Beech Park Home perhaps. I knew how she'd feel about that; she'd rather be dead! But nobody would ask me, would they? I mean, I was just the servant. I thought that if only I could just tide things over for a bit until she got back to her old self or . . . well, until she died in her own home . . . Perhaps there were other things I could have done,' Nancy's face was bleak, 'but I was at my wit's end; I don't suppose I was thinking very straight. I'm just trying to explain how it seemed to me at the time. I'm not trying to make excuses for what I did – there aren't any really.'

'Just take your time, Nancy,' Alice heard herself saying, sounding, she thought, like a detective in a cheap crime story. Crime? Nancy? she asked herself, wondering if perhaps she ought to have followed Mr Appleyard's advice to 'leave well alone'.

'Well, one day it struck me that there were all these useless things around the house. They must be worth quite a bit, I thought, what with people always ready to pay good money for antique knick-knacks. It wasn't as if Miss Sophie could even enjoy looking at them any more, with her being stuck upstairs in bed. What was the good of all that stuff of your grandfather's just lying around collecting dust while I couldn't even keep Miss Sophie warm, couldn't even buy her the kind of nice tasty food she needed to tempt her appetite? A lot of things had been put out of sight anyway, in cupboards and boxes. I'd helped Miss Sophie to do that when her mother became bedridden; it cut down on the dusting when we had more than enough to do without that. "It's not as though she'll notice," Miss Sophie had said.'

Nancy needed no prompting now. She was talking very quickly, eager to have everything said before, perhaps, her resolve failed her.

'Fred still came off and on to keep the garden straight. I was paying him out of my own savings by then. Him being around meant that I could get out to do the shopping – he'd pop upstairs, you see, and check that she was all right when I was out. She liked seeing Fred, thought the world of him, she did. Anyway. So, the next time he came, I took something into Tern Bay to see if I could raise some money on it from the man who'd taken over the old antique shop. With him being new to the village he wouldn't know who I was, wouldn't twig anything odd, I thought. What I took was a little table lamp, one of the ones that Miss Sophie had put away. It was that one that looked as though its wooden stand was really made out of bamboo, the shade was painted with bamboo and leaves, quite nice really. I don't suppose you remember it, there being so many table lamps in the house.'

'But I do – you mean the Tiffany lamp!'

'That's the one. Well he took a good look at it, then he checked up in some book in the back room. He came back and offered me £150 for it – jut like that, no haggling, cash put down on the table. Easy as that! My word, I'd found the right answer to the problem, I thought. I'd never expected that much just for a table lamp. I mean, it's not as though electric stuff is even antique, is it? So then I asked him if he'd be interested in buying anything else. He asked me what I had in mind. So I said almost anything as long as it wasn't big like furniture: ivory figures, vases, little china ornaments and those little bits of green stuff, jade, isn't it? I must be quite a collector, he said. Then he asked if he could come to see the stuff I wanted to sell, he said that would be the best thing. Well, that was a bit of a facer! He'd have to be told where I lived. And what if Miss Sophie heard his car? And what if he arrived when the doctor was here, or the nurse or someone like that? So I said for him not to bother; I'd just bring in something now and again when I came in for the shopping.

'But he became sort of insistent; very nice with it but he wouldn't let it drop. And, what's more, he'd put his hand, sort of casual, on the money which was still on the table. All of a sudden it struck me that perhaps he thought that I was stealing things. I suppose I was, really, but not in the way he would be thinking. I could feel myself getting all flustered and my face going red. So I had to tell him something – well, I had to, hadn't I? I was afraid that with me looking so guilty like, he might call the police! He'd smelt a rat and no mistake . . . well, I suppose that in that line of country they come up against all sorts of crooks so they're on their guard. I could have kicked myself, really I could!'

'So what did you tell him?'

'Well, a story came to me all pat, as it were. Honestly, I was quite surprised at myself. "O what a tangled web we weave . . ." I told him that the lady I worked for was in some financial difficulty and wanted to raise some cash by selling a few things that she'd no use for. She'd be embarrassed, I said, if it got around and she'd be glad if he didn't put the lamp on sale locally for fear anybody might recognise it and get wind of what she was having to do. Then what did he do but ask if he could have her name and the telephone number so that he could speak to her himself! I said that he couldn't do that as she was bedridden and couldn't reach the telephone but I'd give her his message and telephone him back if she wanted him to visit and look at her things. Then I thought that maybe that made it sound more suspicious but, funnily enough, he seemed to accept it. Tell her, he said, that he'd visit her very discreetly, in the evening if that suited her, and he'd be careful not to park right outside the house so that the neighbours wouldn't notice. Well, of course, it's not as if we've got near neighbours here, but he wasn't to know that. But him saying that made me sure that he had no idea where I lived and that was some comfort. He took his hand off the money then and sort of nudged it nearer me. Well, I was so relieved, I can tell you!

'I suppose it was me being sort of off the hook that put me off-guard, because when he smiled and said, "Right then, you'll phone me back and tell me what your employer says. What did you say her name was?" "Miss Cutler," said I, without thinking. I couldn't believe I'd be that stupid; but then, I'm not really cut out for that sort of thing. Anyway, he smiled and said something, smooth as you like, about how I was to tell Miss Cutler that he was looking forward to doing business with her. He's got a lovely voice, you know, that Mr Fellowes! But for all that, I knew he'd tricked me. If I didn't get in touch again, he might start asking around. It wouldn't be difficult for him to find out that I came from Fernhurst, what with Miss Cutler being the only one of that name in the telephone book. The fat would be fairly in the fire, I thought!'

'What did you decide to do?'

'Well, Nurse came that afternoon. A very nice girl, she is, very gentle. She used to come to lend a hand when your grandmother was dying, so she knew Miss Sophie and myself. After your aunt's stroke, the doctor arranged for her to make visits, to check Miss Sophie wasn't getting bedsores – as though I'd let such a thing happen! But I suppose they have to keep an eye on things. Sometimes she needed to give her an enema and other times she'd show her exercises to do in bed, that sort of thing.'

'You confided in her?' Alice hoped her voice did not betray her impatience.

'Goodness, no! Of course she knew Miss Sophie had changed a lot – well, knowing her as she was before, she couldn't but notice that. But she didn't know the half of it, about her being so odd about money and so forth. I wasn't going to be disloyal and discuss Miss Sophie's funny ways with her; I didn't think intimate things like that were her business at all. Oh no! Anyway, she stopped for a cup of tea and she must have noticed that I was looking worried, tired too, I shouldn't wonder. She said perhaps it would be best after all if I took the doctor's advice and let Miss Sophie go into hospital and that I must think of myself too – things like that. But, of course, she soon saw that I wouldn't hear of trying to push that idea on to Miss Sophie. Her place was in her own home with me and that's where she wanted to be, I told her. So then she said that she understood how I felt and that she believed that I wouldn't have to struggle on much longer as Miss Sophie's heart was getting weaker and how it would be a release for both of us . . . So that made up my mind for me. I decided that I'd just have to convince the antiques man that everything was above-board and then sell some more things to him to raise as much money as I needed to keep things running like they should until it wouldn't matter any more.'

Alice, her mouth dry, took a sip of the cold dregs in her cup. 'And did you convince him?'

'I must have. Leastways, it seemed like I had. I telephoned him in the evening, after Miss Sophie had had her pill and was sound asleep. I asked him to come round one evening and to come to the back door. Then, when he came, I told him the truth of it. Well, honesty is the best policy in the end – isn't it?

'He just listened and didn't ask any more questions. Didn't ask to see anything that night but said he'd be back one evening later in the week and told me to promise not to approach any other dealers.

'He came a few times after that. Do you know, I used to look forward to seeing him. I can't tell you how comforting he was, ever so kind. Or it seemed like that. He'd move around the drawing room, quiet as the cat, looking at this and that. Then he'd pick on one or two little things, nothing that seemed all that special, really, and he'd give me ever such good prices. Far more, at least, that I would expect, not that I knew much about it. He'd ask me how much I really needed and then find something that would fetch whatever it was. I'll tell you one thing he bought: that white china hand that your grandmother used to have on her dressing table for rings. Do you remember it?' Nancy held up her hand, fingers slightly curled; thin fingers that trembled a little, the back of her hand mottled with the liver blotches of age.

Alice, silent, nodded.

'Your aunt hated that thing!' Nancy laughed a little, remembering. 'Said it made her think of a dead hand reaching out from the grave! She'd put it away in that wall cupboard in the morning room after your grandmother died. Do you know, he gave me two hundred pounds for that – just fancy! I paid the electricity bill, then the rates and the telephone, and still hardly a dent made in all that store of stuff. He was always so nice – we got quite close in a way . . .' Nancy mused.

Alice waited.

'We'd have coffee here in the kitchen; with the door closed we could talk without fear of Miss Sophie hearing, not that she was likely to wake up after taking her sleeping pill. I'd put the coffee on, he'd fetch the cups . . . the sugar-bowl, he admired that bowl. Quite at home, he was, and always so very kind. He's a godsend, I remember thinking!' Nancy sighed.

Nancy was so absorbed in her own recall of the past that she seemed oblivious of Alice's presence. For that, Alice was at least grateful.

'Then one day the lamp on Miss Sophie's bedside table went phut. She told me to bring up another. When I did, she said it wasn't the one she wanted. She wanted the Tiffany lamp, she said. She remembered the cupboard she'd put it in, too. I pretended to look for it and told her I could-n't find it. She got in a great state and sent me off to look for it again. Then I tried telling her that I'd just remem-bered that it had needed rewiring and with one thing and another I'd forgotten to collect it from the electrical shop. But in the end . . . well, as I said, I'm not much good at that sort of thing.

'Anyway, in the end I told her what I'd done. I didn't tell her everything, only about the lamp. It was awful. She did-n't storm; she was icy, contemptuous. That was at first. Then she cried a bit about how I was the last friend she had, the one person she thought she could trust and how could I thieve from her, deceive her.' The tears were coursing down Nancy's face, unheeded.

'I tried to take her in my arms, comfort her. But she pushed me away. She said . . .' Nancy fell silent, her mouth ugly in her attempt to get her lips under control to tell what she seemed compelled to tell. Alice tried to say something but Nancy held up her hand and continued after a pause, her voice unsteady.

'She said a lot of things. By the next day she was different again. She became very calm and told me that she was going to change her will because what I'd done was beyond forgiving. I told her that I accepted that. She wasn't going to leave me a penny, she said, as, for all she knew, I'd been feathering my own nest for years. She actually said that!' There was a look of guileless wonder on Nancy's face.

'Funnily enough, she didn't seem upset any more, sort of collected, she was, calm inside herself now that she had decided what she wanted to do. Do you know, I almost felt better, too, knowing she'd have the satisfaction of doing what she thought was the just thing. That may not make sense to you – in a way, it doesn't really make sense to me either, but that's how it was. It was a bit like when a little child kicks you because he's broken his toy; you know he just has to get it out somehow. Really we were both very calm about it by that time. Besides, none of it seemed real, I still couldn't quite believe any of it was happening.

'Then she wrote to the solicitor – old Mr Appleyard – instructing him to draw up a new will and telling him when to bring it for her signature. She told me what she'd written and then put it under her pillow and told me to send Fred to her – it was one of his days for the garden. When he came downstairs he had the letter ready stamped in his hand. She didn't trust me to post it . . .'

Nancy covered her face with her hands and began to rock to and fro in her chair.

Alice rose to her feet clumsily. The muscles which she had held clenched and tense responded sluggishly and she felt as she sometimes had in a nightmare when her body would fail to respond to her command. Stiffly she walked to the dining room. She returned with a glass of brandy. She put her arms round Nancy and cajoled her to drink.

Nancy uncovered her face, stared dubiously at the glass. She lifted it to her lips and quaffed the brandy in one gulp like a child swallowing disagreeable medicine. She gasped, coughed, tears running freely now down her cheeks.

'Nancy, you must promise me that you will put the whole dreadful story out of your mind. You did what you thought was right in a difficult situation. Poor Sophie was clearly not in her right mind; neither of you was responsible . . . You were loyal and loving to her right to the end, I know that. Often when people grow confused in their minds, particularly elderly people, they turn against those they love the most – that's well-known. It's a sort of paranoia. Now, you're not to worry over it any more and I'm going to put right the injustice she did to you over the money . . .'

'It's not the money that matters!' Nancy wailed. 'Don't you understand that?'

'Of course I do. But at least it is one thing that can be put right. And it must be, for Sophie's sake as well as your own.'

Nancy blew her nose, blotted her tears.

'That's better! It's over and done with, Nancy. We won't ever talk about it again and you're to stop brooding over it. Promise?'

'But there's more . . .'

Dear God, hasn't there been enough! thought Alice, a

dreadful anguished weariness preventing her from saying anything that would stop Nancy from making another shocking revelation. She reflected that in a letter the matter of greatest import was often conveyed in the postscript, the hope of the writer presumably being that, under the guise of it being no more than an afterthought, its real significance would in some way be obscured. In dread, she waited.

'The lady I'm with now is a great one for exhibitions. Paintings, antiques, that sort of thing. We were at an antique fair and I saw the very spit of that lamp. She saw me staring at it – well, it brought everything back. "My Miss Cutler had a lamp, just like that," I said, in case she wondered why I was so fixed on it. She said that my last employer must have been very rich indeed as that lamp was worth thousands. I thought perhaps she'd got it wrong so I asked one of the young gentlemen running things how much it was worth. He said over £10,000, on account of it being a Tiffany. Just think of that, then! And him being such a gentleman and so nice, that Mr Fellowes – oh, he could charm the birds off the trees, that one. He must have been laughing up his sleeve – and me being afraid he might take me for a villain!'

'Yes. Well – as I said, Nancy, you mustn't brood over any of it any more; you said yourself that the money was not what mattered.' Alice's voice was controlled. Please, please, she prayed, let me keep calm until I am alone. Later I must bear to think – but not now, please.

'I'll make us a fresh pot of tea,' said Alice, her voice light, just as though something fragile and very precious had not been irrevocably smashed.

'No, you sit where you are!' Nancy had risen from the table. 'Let me – it's not as though I don't know where everything is; you've hardly changed a thing.'

Alice tried to banish from her mind the memory of Paul so unerringly locating the sugar bowl. Strange that the table bore nothing but the tray, china, the prim cakestand; she almost expected it to be aglint with shattered crystal, sharp glittering splinters, long enough to pierce through flesh.

Nancy made tea, rinsed out their cups, tidied the table. Was it the brandy or the cathartic effect of confession that held such curative powers? Alice wondered, but could not find it in herself to begrudge Nancy her recovery.

Later they walked in the garden. April danced on the lawn, her deft paws batting the air but never quite striking down the butterfly that fluttered just beyond her reach.

Alice plucked flowers for Nancy to take home as a gift for Maud. She gathered dahlias, selecting only those of the large cactus type which she particularly disliked, huge puce-coloured blooms, their petals like the tentacles of some monstrous sea-anemone. Alice could visualise them on Maud's dining table, drooping dourly over the beetroot and brawn, the ham and piccalilli.

'Oh yes, Maud'll love these!' said Nancy, exchanging a conspiratorial smile.

'Just think, Nancy, once you've got a little income of your own, you can retire whenever you want to and live quite independently of Maud. How happy dear Sophie would be if she knew that it would all turn out all right in the end. Perhaps she does know.'

The bus that Nancy had planned to catch had long since gone. Alice drove her home and welcomed the necessity that postponed the moment when she would be alone, her mind undistracted, powerless to resist dwelling upon the full implications of what she had learned.

As they drove past Le Bijou, Mary, brandishing a pair of shears, waved to them. She was perched precariously on a step-ladder on the verge of the road and was clipping the thicket of shrubs that towered above her garden wall.

'Nice for you to have an old friend so near – is Mr Burton still in the house with her? Miss Sophie was very fond of her, you know. We'd call in sometimes if we were out on one of our little walks; gave your aunt the chance of a little rest and a sit-down.

'Did Miss Sophie ever tell you about the time when we called in on one boiling hot day and we found her painting in the garden with absolutely nothing on but a pair of skimpy panties? No? Well, it was the strangest thing – you'll never guess what she was painting! She'd rigged up a hammock between two apple trees and Mr Burton was stretched out in it dressed in a dark business suit – you know the kind I mean – and a rolled umbrella and a bunch of red balloons were hung on the branches over his head. Well, you couldn't help but laugh! Your aunt said that that was what's called surrealist art. What a sight – and her just in her panties!'

Alice laughed and then found to her horror that what had started as no more than a polite response to Nancy's story had taken on a life of its own, had become a wild, gasping cacophony that blinded her eyes with tears and shook the steering wheel under her hands with its force. Only Nancy's sudden grasp of the wheel saved them from weaving into the path of an oncoming van.

That strange frightening laughter abruptly quelled by the near collision, Alice glanced at Nancy's face and its sudden pallor, coupled with the sight of the bouquet of hideous dahlias on her lap, sobered her completely.

'Well, perhaps it wasn't all *that* funny,' she said sheepishly.

'I expect you're just a bit over-wrought. And little wonder! I shouldn't have burdened you with the whole story, but you've no idea what a relief it's been to me to get it all off my chest at long last. But it was selfish of me, easing my own mind at someone else's expense. And it *has* been at your expense, Miss Alice. When I think about that lamp, I could—'

'To hell with the bloody lamp!' Alice bawled. 'We agreed that none of it would be mentioned, ever again. O.K., O.K. you did a damned silly thing but we all behave like idiots from time to time. I should know! At least you've made a fool of yourself out of the best of intentions. Just give it a rest. No one's blaming you. I forgive you – I'm sure Sophie, wherever she is, forgives you. Except that there's nothing for her *to* forgive as far as you're concerned. So now will you just shut up about it, once and for all. For God's sake just bloody well shut up!'

Shocked, Nancy remained silent for the rest of the short journey. But the farewells were accomplished decently enough, Alice once more gentle, Nancy wary.

She thinks I'm going barmy like my aunt before me, and perhaps I am, thought Alice, watching Nancy, scattering petals as she went, bolting up the path to her sister's door at a speed which could scarcely be attributed to a longing to be reunited with Maud.

I'll write her a nice letter, Alice promised herself, when I've sorted myself out, got myself up off the ground. If I ever do.

The telephone was ringing as Alice entered the hall at Fernhurst. It was Miss Vine's voice at the other end; disguising her own, Alice snapped 'wrong number' and, replacing the receiver, vented a colourful suggestion as to what Miss Vine might well do with herself. She was a little surprised at her command of an alternative form of self-expression which she could not recall having ever consciously acquired.

Her hands were clenching and unclenching, apparently of their own volition. Her legs seemed filled with an urge for violent action. She strode restlessly and aimlessly from room to room, flinging wide the doors, slamming them shut behind her and all the time pursued by the insistent clamour of the telephone as, presumably, Miss Vine stubbornly persisted in redialling.

Alice escaped outside, where dusk was already seeping into the garden, stealing like a mist over the lawn. A hedgehog scurried across her path with a surprising turn of speed, looking like an old lady lifting her skirts and fleeing from something very nasty.

The scent of the last of summer's flowers, the quiet, the soft glimmer of blossoms slow to surrender their colour to the gathering dusk exerted a calming influence which Alice tried to resist. She was fearful of allowing the heat of her rage to cool, sensing that the black doltish slugs of shame and self-pity awaited only the dying of the fire to slither forth to munch and destroy her already wounded self-respect.

How could I have allowed myself to be so taken in by such a calculating scoundrel? Oh the humiliations to which women expose themselves to assuage their hunger to have a man in their lives!

But at least I didn't offer to lend him money; he wasted his wiles there, Alice reminded herself. Discarding nothing that might add fuel to the flame, she remembered her Rosenthal and mourned its loss. She imagined Paul saying something witty to Simon about its acquisition: 'one of my little trophies!' Most likely he'd already sold it. She remembered the melting delight with which she had watched Paul's slim sensitive fingers caress the cherries, the grapes, the damsons, embossed in gentle misty-blue upon each plate. 'Sod him!' she shouted, startling a dozing blackbird out of its wits so that it rose from a laurel bush clattering alarm and setting off a score of panicked rustlings, furtive susurrations in the shadowy undergrowth.

Sobered by the fierceness of her own reaction and not a little shamed, Alice stood quite still for some minutes, the night air cool on her face and, as silence was gradually restored to the garden, she experienced a like calm creep over herself. She resumed her pacing up and down and across the lawn, but now her stride was shorter, slower, each footfall deliberate, almost apologetic.

She had, she admonished herself, blundered through the summer like a sleepwalker. Now, abruptly awakened, she found herself suddenly in strange territory and from the unfamiliar vantage point thus afforded had discovered that the landscape through which she had earlier travelled, and which at the time she had believed she had understood, had subtly changed; even the figures which populated it she now saw from an altered angle and found they no longer quite accorded with her original conception of them.

But one landmark remained unchanged, was instantly recognisable, and that was the place on her path at which she had been deprived of the staff on which she had been accustomed to lean for the greater part of her journey. That significant point in her travel now appeared to be only a hand's breadth away – which surprised her, as she had come to believe that she had already progressed much further from it. She now realised that while she had certainly moved away from that point, she had, in fact, been travelling not forward but back along the track and finally had wandered off it altogether. She had missed her way, her eyes on the ground, her sense of direction lost as she had searched frantically for a replacement for the support that death had wrenched from her hand.

But surely, Alice told herself, she had been deluded in thinking herself incapable of continuing on her journey alone and unsupported; if she was indeed incapable, then she could not now be standing so firm and strong and with such a clear view of the route upon which she had travelled. She must find the confidence to turn her back on the vista of the past and find the courage to go forward, secure in the knowledge that she need no longer devote her energies, restrict her vision, to the search for another staff upon which to lean. Who knows, she thought, I may even stumble upon one lying across my path; but it will be a matter of choice, not compulsion, whether or not I stretch out my hand to take it.

It would be unrealistic to suppose that there would be no twists and turns to negotiate on the way ahead, no sudden obstacles, no surprises lying in wait to challenge her stamina, her ingenuity and resilience. I must be prepared for anything, Alice told herself, suddenly strong in her rediscovered self-confidence. I may even persuade myself to welcome the challenge of the unexpected because, without that, life could degenerate into nothing more entertaining than a predictable plod from starting line to finishing post and surely no one would wish for that!

Conscious of the moistness in the air, the grass striking chill through her sandals, Alice turned towards the house. Light spilled from the kitchen window and through the wide-open door lighting her way. A low shadow, only faintly lighter than the darker shadows from which it detached itself, moved swiftly across the lawn to her side. April, returning from her own secret preoccupations, rubbed herself against Alice's legs, her long tail held high, her fur cool and damp with the dew of evening.

The cat rushed eagerly ahead into the beckoning shaft of

light that pointed the way to warmth and supper. Quickening her pace, Alice followed in her wake, her mind now firmly focussed on the present.

There could be no question now, she decided, but that when Paul returned he would find her ready and waiting for his farewell visit.

9
~

How, Alice wondered, could she ever have attributed Paul's habit when speaking of rarely meeting one's eye to an endearing shyness in his nature? It was clearly an obvious indication that he was a shifty character. His ears were decidedly odd too: no lobes to speak of. Chair tilted back, eyes fixed on the ceiling, he was telling her about his recent trip with Simon, highlighting amusing incidents; at least, he seemed to think they were amusing. The comb of honey which he had brought her from Devon lay on a plate between them on the kitchen table.

She was finding it less difficult than she had feared to be pleasant to him, not to betray the revulsion she felt. It helped to know that she need only sustain for, at most, a couple of hours this act of pretending that nothing had changed. Paul would, as he had explained, be leaving for France early the following morning and still had a great deal to do in preparation for that departure so his visit must, of necessity, be short.

'I'll make some tea in a moment but, first, I wonder if you could do me a favour?'

'Nothing would give me greater pleasure!' he replied, righting his chair, bringing his eyes into direct contact with her own and favouring her with one of his warm smiles which she had always found so charming.

'It's just that I wonder if you could pull down the ladder that gives access to the loft; there's a pulley contraption which I'd rather not have to manage on my own. I was going to wait until Fred comes for his stint in the garden tomorrow, but as you're here, perhaps you could give me a hand.'

As he followed her up the stairs to the top landing, Alice explained that Clare was looking for props for an amateur production to be presented in the church hall and had asked her if she could provide a couple of tennis racquets of pre-war vintage. As nothing in Fernhurst seemed ever to have been thrown away, Alice was sure that discarded racquets must be mouldering still in the attic.

She expressed wonder at his competence as Paul manipulated the ropes which opened the trapdoor above their heads and then hauled down the ladder. Paul went through the performance that men feel impelled to carry out when presented with a ladder: he gave it a shake or two, applied a sharp downward pull to a couple of the rungs and pronounced himself satisfied as to its sturdiness. Alice, after a certain show of reluctance, allowed herself to be persuaded that it would be as well if she mounted the ladder now while there was someone with her to help carry down the racquets and guide her feet on the rungs should her courage fail her on her descent.

Tongue nipped between her teeth, eyes fixed resolutely upward in obedience to Paul's injunction not to look down, Alice ascended and confessed, when Paul had joined her in the attic, that she was so grateful that he'd insisted on being present as she was really rather nervous of heights. It was true that she had found her previous and solitary foray in the attic a nerve-racking affair.

Paul brushed aside her thanks with a perfunctoriness which, she felt, owed more to his eagerness to explore the mysteries of the attic than to modesty about the confidence his presence apparently lent her.

He located and turned on a switch so that the mildewed light which filtered through the cobwebs that shrouded the skylight was augmented by the dim glow of a shadeless bulb that dangled overhead.

'Bother, I ought to have brought a torch!' Alice was peering into the gloom in a vague and uncertain manner. 'I seem to remember an old steamer trunk down this side somewhere; there were all sorts of bits and pieces in it. I remember poking about in it when I was a child. It was a great treat to be allowed up here! Perhaps,' she called out to Paul who was already heading in the direction in which she was looking, 'you could rootle through those tea chests beside that rolled-up carpet over there while I look for the trunk – I half-remember where it ought to be. Do watch your clothes; everything's so filthy!' she added. But Paul, changing direction, was adroitly weaving his way in the half-light between the piles of discarded objects with the skill of one accustomed to finding his way through the cluttered labyrinth of crowded auction rooms.

She had located the trunk and was clearing from its lid a pile of cracked plates, broken-ribbed umbrellas and a pillow-slip filled with old Christmas cards, when she heard Paul's footsteps falter.

'Any luck?' she called as he halted just short of the tea chests. He didn't reply immediately. He was pulling aside an old velour curtain that had been thrown over a thick square shape that leaned against the leg of a wash-stand. Alice, her eyes on Paul, continued to pile the dusty crockery on the attic floor. The clink and rattle of the plates and the chatter of starlings squabbling on the roof above were the only sounds.

'There's a stack of paintings here – unframed,' he said, at last.

'Really? They're probably Aunt Sophie's. Wait a mo . . .' Alice made her way to where Paul stooped, fingering his way through the canvases, occasionally withdrawing one and peering at it in the drizzled light.

'Yes, those are Sophie's frightful daubs! She brought them back from Paris after her stint at a finishing school there. Had the good sense never to frame any of them, thank God!'

Paul's fingers had stopped their riffling through the pictures. 'How extraordinary!' he said, lifting clear the vividly coloured canvas that had arrested his attention.

Alice moved nearer. 'Well, that's certainly not one that Aunt Sophie painted!'

Paul carried the canvas over to the skylight, turned it over, brushed a rope of grimy cobweb from its back and peered at the Parisian colourman's faded label that was still. glued to the stretcher.

'She was in Paris in the twenties, wasn't she – your aunt?'

'That's right. As far as painting went, it was obviously a sheer waste of time and money. But even Aunt Sophie can't be blamed for that horror – what's it meant to be, do you suppose?'

Paul wasn't listening. He was holding the canvas at arm's length, gazing at it with concentrated appraisal. Alice thought she detected a faint smile but in the poor light couldn't be certain. The cat that swallowed the cream, she thought, fairly certain that she had glimpsed on his face a quickly suppressed start of surprised recognition. She took a step backward in case her own expression might betray her.

'God, it's stifling up here!' Alice was making her way back to the trunk. 'If we don't find those darned racquets soon, I'm going to call it a day.' Paul, as she could see, had placed

the picture with some care on a bundle of old magazines. 'I'll
have a look in the tea chests,' he offered.

'Hold on, no need to bother.' Alice had succeeded in
clearing and lifting the lid of the trunk and was triumphantly
brandishing two ancient racquets locked in their wooden
presses. 'It seems almost an act of treachery, lending the poor
old things to Clare; I bet her play will be all about the deca-
dence of the privileged classes in the twenties!'

She was standing now by the open trapdoor, looking
with an air of dubiety at the Heath Robinson–ish device that
served to raise and lower lumber between the attic and the
floor below. 'D'you think their frames might split if I just
drop them down?'

Paul had found an old haversack and suggested it would
be better if he slung that over his shoulders and carried the
racquets down in it. When they had been stowed in the
haversack, he added, 'Do you mind if I take that painting
down too? I'd like to see it in a decent light.'

'Go ahead.' Alice's tone was off-hand. 'Although it looks
ghastly enough in half-light, if you ask me.'

Downstairs, they washed their hands, side by side at the
kitchen sink; like children called in from play, thought Alice.
Paul had rolled up his shirt sleeves and it struck her that his
wristwatch was ostentatiously expensive. In an earlier time,
she thought, lowering her eyes to hide their contemptuous
gleam, his kind would have been flaunting a gold cigarette
case. I would have noticed all these pointers in time, she
assured herself: the ears, the watch and even that melliflu-
ous voice which she now suspected was deliberately
cultivated – not a natural attribute as it had been in her dear
Oliver's case. How could she ever have compared Paul to
Oliver . . .? There had been a moment, she told herself
grimly, when I could cheerfully have pushed him down
through the open hatch; and she almost believed it.

Paul had propped the picture on the dresser, where it now rested in almost the identical position in which Mary had placed it on the day she had given it to Alice.

'Do you know,' said Alice, bringing the teapot to the table, 'looking at that painting in full light, I can see it could have its attractions.' Head slightly tilted, she stared at it reflectively. 'It's the sort of thing that my son might like – I must remember to show it to him when he comes down. I could give it to him for his birthday.'

'Mmm. On the other hand, he might accept it only because he wouldn't want to offend you.' Paul's gaze was fixed on the canvas, one hand gently massaging his chin.

Alice's tone was light. 'I don't think David is all that concerned about not injuring my feelings.' She glanced at Paul. 'Gracious! Don't tell me you have taken a fancy to it yourself?'

'Actually, I have rather.'

'Goodness, Paul, you do surprise me! What is it that you like about it – I wouldn't have thought that it was your sort of thing.'

'Finding it like that – among those other pictures – well, that intrigues me. So very surprising! There is something very puzzling – oh, I find it difficult to explain.' Paul hesitated, not looking at Alice. When she remained silent, he continued, 'Let's just say that I think it would be proper if that picture belonged to someone who would really like to have it.'

'Are you speaking now as a dealer or does it appeal to you personally? I say, you don't imagine, do you, that it's been painted by someone important in that sort of genre?'

'Goodness, no! The appeal is purely personal. Frankly, I'd just like to have it.'

Alice made no reply but sat, apparently bemused, staring at the picture. 'Well,' she said at last, 'if you'd *really* like to have it . . .' she hesitated. This, she thought, must be what an angler feels when the fish has taken the fly; dare I pay out more line and play it a little longer or ought I to strike now in case he gets away? She was aware that Paul was watching her, but with an expression which she could not quite fathom.

'Would you be frightfully offended if I made you an offer?'

Alice laughed, 'Do people really say that – well, I suppose they must!'

'I assure you that I'm being perfectly serious. You don't like the picture. I do. So why not sell it and buy something which you'd be happy to have?'

'But selling something to a friend – well, it doesn't seem quite right.'

'Nonsense, Alice! Why shouldn't one transact business with someone one knows – in fact, I'd have thought it the most satisfactory way to go about things.'

Alice rose and picked up the canvas. She held it out towards Paul.

'You like it, you have it!'

'Now you're embarrassing *me*, Alice. I want to buy it – in fact I insist on paying for it.' Paul took out his cheque-book. 'What do you say to a hundred quid?'

Alice looked at him with an expression which she hoped would convey slight bewilderment.

'No, a hundred and fifty would be fairer.' Paul was unscrewing the top from his pen.

'Oh, I wasn't quibbling. It was just that I thought a hundred pounds seems an awful lot for it. But then I know simply nothing about the value of paintings. I'm entirely in your hands.'

Paul was already scribbling a cheque. 'I assure you, that's the price I'd offer, regardless of who the seller was.'

'Well, if you're sure – but it doesn't seem worth that to me.'

'It is to me,' said Paul, taking the picture from her.

'Here,' he said, fishing in the pocket of his jacket. 'I'll make out a proper duplicated receipt just to convince you that I am treating it as I would any business done in the shop and not giving you any more than I honestly think it's worth. That convince you?' he asked, handing her the completed receipt.

He really is good at it, thought Alice with a certain wondering respect. If a seller later suspected she'd been diddled, he could always produce his copy of the receipt in support of it having been a perfectly properly conducted and therefore irreversible transaction. Poor Nancy hadn't stood a chance!

'Oh you really shouldn't have bothered with that, Paul. I just wouldn't like you to pay over the odds. I do think it is so truly awful when people take advantage – it's something I feel strongly about. Goodness, it does seem odd, taking money from you!' Alice placed the cheque under the sugar-bowl and poured their tea.

Paul glanced at his watch and added more milk to cool his tea. 'I really must be off in a minute, Alice. I've still a helluva lot to do if I'm to get away on schedule tomorrow, you know how it is.'

Alice nodded. Only a little longer to go, she comforted herself, setting her face into an expression of regret suitable to his departure.

They made their adieux outside on the drive. Paul, having placed the canvas with some care on the back seat of his car, stood beside its open door and Alice suffered a peck on her cheek and assurances that he'd look her up at some unspecified time in the future.

'I've just thought – oughtn't I to give you a thing, a

what's-its-name about the picture? You know, the seller's account of its past history, that sort of thing?'

'A certificate of provenance, you mean? Well yes, I suppose that might be an idea, particularly as the canvas is unsigned; not that I've any intention of selling it, but it might be amusing to have some sort of account . . . it'll serve too as an unusual memento, I suppose. It'll do later, no hurry.'

'I'll tell you what, I could send it on to you.'

'Sure, if that's what you'd prefer.' Paul hastily scrawled an address on a page torn from his diary. 'That'll be my base while I'm in France.'

Alice did her best to restrict her smile to one of seemly proportions as she waved him goodbye. But, to her own bewilderment, she found herself compelled to turn away before she could watch him disappear completely from her sight.

I deceived only by omission, Alice told herself, feeling smugly satisfied with the afternoon's performance. Paul, she recalled, had employed the same stratagem. When she had tried to establish a rational reason for his knowledge of the location of the sugar-bowl (how ridiculous all *that* seemed now!) he had truthfully answered the only question she had thought to put to him when he had told her that he had never met her aunt. He had clearly intended her to attach some mystical significance to the event.

Her indignation refuelled, Alice fixed her attention once more on the sheet of paper under her hand. She had completed the first paragraph of the account of the painting's history, having rendered a fair description of its appearance and continued with details of the date and place of her sale of it to Paul Fellowes. Composing the second paragraph was a pleasure not to be hurried. Finally, she wrote:

This unsigned picture was gifted to me by its
painter, Miss Mary Bowles of Le Bijou, Tern
Bay. Miss Bowles painted the picture (in the style
of Piet Mondrian) over an existing picture given
to her by myself. Under Miss Bowles's work is a
picture of a bowl of marigolds which was painted
in Paris at some time in the early nineteen-
twenties by my aunt (the late Miss Sophie
Cutler). Miss Bowles executed her painting in
the summer of this year.

Alice dated and signed the sheet of paper. She folded the
sheet with neat precision, the creases sharp and crisp, and
slipped it into the envelope on which she had written the
address that Paul had given her. In the morning she would
post it.

She then wrote a brief note to Mary.

Hope you won't be offended, but I've sold your
painting to someone who seemed awfully keen to
have it. £150 – not bad?

She attached a cheque to the note. She would slip the envelope through Mary's letterbox on her way to Tern Bay in
the morning and trust that Mary would not see her. She
was uncertain as yet as to how much she should confide to
Mary but was aware that the temptation to recount how she
had served Paul with his come-uppance might prove too
strong to resist.

It would be comforting to believe that Barbara, Thelma
and Mary were all unaware of how often she had been in
Paul's company and, better still, to be able to believe that if
ever in possession of the whole story they would be
wickedly amused – but not at her expense. Better to be

wary, to play it by ear, Alice decided. If Paul was mentioned, she would look knowing, might let drop that she'd given him the occasional meal when his flat was invaded by the builders. Well, most women, she would imply, would take pity on a man in such circumstances. A hint could be dropped that, personally, she had found him rather dull.

Of course it was a shame that he should escape prosecution for dealing in stolen goods. The way he had taken advantage of Nancy's misguided ploy and her ignorance over the value of the Tiffany lamp didn't bear thinking about. The money she had tricked him out of was small beer compared to the thumping profit he must have made on that one transaction alone. But financial recompense had not been her motivation. To set the law in motion was quite out of the question. It would certainly land Nancy in trouble, and her own involvement with Paul (she could just hear some smug legal pundit describe it as 'an infatuation') would doubtless emerge. Besides, it would be most distasteful to have poor Sophie's eccentric behaviour made a topic for public discussion, particularly after Nancy had gone to such disastrous lengths to avoid just such a turn of events.

In the days that had elapsed since Nancy's visit, Alice had put in train the arrangements that would ensure Nancy had a suitably generous annuity. Now all that remained to be done was for her to keep an appointment with Mr Appleyard in the morning to sign the relevant documents.

Alice tidied and closed her bureau. She rather looked forward to the morning. A wind was getting up, blowing in from the sea, dissipating the sultry warmth of the September day, breaking the somnolent stillness, carrying with it a fresh invigoration.

She sat quietly, although none too comfortably, on the straight-backed chair in front of the bureau. Abstractedly she rubbed her cardiganed forearm across the gleaming rosewood, effacing her fingerprints from its lid. It was time, she thought, for her to put her mind to engaging some domestic help. She could tolerate it now; the invasion of her privacy, the presence of a stranger in Fernhurst. She might invite old friends down for an occasional visit, even to stay for a few days. She thought that she was ready to face that now, would no longer find their presence a cruel reminder of Oliver's absence, herself perhaps for them no longer an embarrassment, a living reminder of mortality. 'What a wonderful idea – make a fresh start, Alice!' they had said, their faces eager with what might have been no more than relief when she had confided her plans to move to Fernhurst. She didn't blame them; they might even have been right. It wasn't easy, it took time, learning how to be more than only a relict – and even more time for those who had known one only as one half of a pair to alter their conception.

Her gaze idly roaming over the drawing room brought Alice little of immediate comfort: the neatness, the orderliness, the plumped cushions, the undisturbed smooth pile of the carpet, the white chrysanthemums standing straight and prim in their crystal vase, struck a chill note. It's like a deserted stage, she thought: the play has finished its run, the cast have taken their last bow and only the set remains.

It's up to me to dismantle it, Alice thought, and suddenly realised how much she looked forward to doing just that.

10
~

The pavements no longer clogged with dawdling holiday-makers, space and to spare in the car park, no queues in the shops, Alice finished her business in Tern Bay quicker than she had dared hope. The letter to Paul had been posted, that for Mary left at Le Bijou without Mary having caught sight of her.

The wind had gathered in strength overnight and, fresh from its unobstructed race across the open sea, it blew bois-terously down the narrow streets, whipping from the litter-bins crisp-bags and ice-cream papers, bowling empty drink cans along the gutters and raising spirals of grit at every corner. Unable to keep a foothold on the chimney pots, the seagulls mewed in indignation, tossing and swoop-ing like scraps of paper over the roofs, their peevish cries all but drowned by the bluster of the wind. On its last day, September, the month when growth and decay seemed equally suspended, was being routed with a vigour which seemed, literally, to snatch one's breath away.

Sheltering in the entrance of the amusement arcade, her head scarf tied firmly under her chin, Alice scanned the page torn from the telephone pad on which she had jotted down Miss Vine's shopping list. If Miss Vine had deliberately set out to ensure that Alice would be required to visit practically every shop in Tern Bay in order to satisfy her needs (always presented as being urgent), she could not have bettered her list, thought Alice, more in resignation than in anger. Her check confirmed that every purchase had been made – a card of knicker elastic, two fillets of plaice, one typewriter ribbon, one pair of black shoe laces, a small bottle of aspirins, four oranges, half a pound of the butcher's own sausages and two dozen first-class stamps. All that remained was to deliver the goods and take the opportunity to vent her indignation at how little had been done by those who had been best placed to discover just what had been going on at Fernhurst towards the end of Sophie's life.

Alice would have liked to fortify herself with a visit to the coffee shop before confronting Miss Vine, but she had glimpsed through its window Barbara and Clare in animated conversation.

From the moment when she had entered Mr Appleyard's office, Alice had known that he was unlikely to offer her a cup of coffee, far less a glass of the excellent sherry with which he occasionally indulged a favoured client. The signs for such a gesture were conspicuously absent, his disapproval barely concealed. His disapproval, Alice suspected, was occasioned not so much by her decision to make financial provision for Nancy, but by the fact that the decision had been arrived at without prior consultation with himself. Mr Appleyard took no pains to disguise his opinion that women were not qualified to manage their own affairs. He grudgingly approved of her choice of an annuity for Nancy in preference to the gift of a lump sum which, he implied, might not only have given Nancy ideas above her proper station but might well have made her the victim of some calculating scoundrel. With that last pronouncement Alice demurely agreed, adding

that it was reassuring to learn that a man of Mr
Appleyard's experience and insights shared her own poor
opinion of the proclivities of his sex. She had been
tempted to add that, considering his lack of confidence in
the ability of women to understand business matters, it
seemed even more reprehensible that he had failed to keep
a closer eye on her aunt's management of her financial
affairs, particularly when she had reached a state of failing
health and advanced age when her judgement might be
thought to be in danger of being impaired. But she had
thought better of it, there being no knowing what self-
righteous steps he might take to shift the burden of
culpability entirely on to the shoulders of Nancy.

Only Miss Vine, Nancy had decided, was to be burdened with the full story of Sophie's sad aberration and the
consequent cruel deception practised upon Nancy by Paul.
There would be no danger that Miss Vine would repeat a
story which reflected so little to her own credit.

'ENTER' commanded the message scrawled on the scrap of
paper that fluttered so frantically to tear itself away from the
drawing pin that impaled it on Miss Vine's front door.

Walking into the sitting room, her eyes not yet adjusted
to the gloom, Alice was startled to discover that what she
had assumed to be a pile of crumpled washing spilling over
the armchair by the fireplace was, in fact, Miss Vine.

Cocooned in a patchwork quilt, her eyes bulbous under
their paper-thin lids, her mouth agape, Miss Vine was
asleep. Her face, poking forth from the enveloping wrap-
pings, was reminiscent of that of a newly hatched bird
rolling over the edge of its nest, sightless, its thin wrinkled
skin too large for the underlying bone structure, little wisps
of hair sprouting on its nakedness and trembling slightly
with every exhalation of breath.

Embarrassed, Alice backed quietly out of the room, closing the door gently behind her. Opening and banging shut the front door, she stamped her feet loudly in the little lobby, calling out 'anybody at home?' before rapping firmly on the sitting room door and, having opened it, poked her head in first in a winsome peek-a-boo manner which set her toes curling with distaste.

'There you are at last! I thought you'd got lost on the way. Gossiping for hours in the coffee-shop, I suppose – oh, I know what you girls are like when you get together.' Miss Vine had pulled herself upright in her chair, had assumed her most queenly expression and was twitching the quilt down from her shoulders; her feet had jerked forward and had come perilously close to kicking over the dusty electric radiator that stood in front of the empty grate. The room smelt of scorched fluff, soot and a hint of menthol rub.

Alice pulled the radiator into a safer position and asked Miss Vine if she was feeling below par.

'Just taking sensible precautions. I may be hatching a cold, and it'd be little wonder with this damned gale blowing. It seems to find its way in through every crack and cranny – look at that!' Miss Vine was pointing to the rug in front of the door, its fringes fluttering perceptibly in the draught. 'No good attempting to light a fire; the smoke just billows out. And to think that there was a time when I used to actually enjoy a high wind – found it exhilarating! My word, how Beech Park used to catch the autumn gales, perched up there on the headland. The girls used to be charged with an extra energy; I'd watch them racing about in the grounds like frisky fillies. One could stand on the cliff and lean into the wind and almost believe that if one stepped off the edge it would toss one back on to the land like a leaf. But now, now I long to cower down before

it like a mouse in the long grass. I must be growing old!'
Miss Vine paused, as though taken unaware by her own
admission.

'Did you get everything on my list?' she asked, brisk
again after her little silence. 'Good! Now be a dear girl and
pop the fish and the sausages in the fridge; just leave the
other things on the dresser and I'll sort them out later.'

'Would you like me to make some coffee?'

'No, not coffee. A pot of tea would be better. Come to
think of it, you could boil me an egg when you're at it;
that'll save me having to bother with preparing a lunch. Do
one for yourself as well, if you like,' she called after Alice as
a generous afterthought.

The neglected state of her kitchen suggested that Miss
Vine was of the opinion that the performance of domestic
chores was unworthy of her attention and the preparation
of meals a tiresome necessity to be performed as perfunc-
torily as possible with a minimum of clearing-up
undertaken afterwards. The only concession to decoration
was a row of dismal cacti which glowered in little pots on
the windowsill and a disintegrating corn dolly nailed to the
larder door – a relic from Clare's brief flirtation with rural
crafts. Shoes occupied the vegetable rack and wizened pota-
toes sprouting long pallid shoots shared a cardboard box on
the floor with a handful of green tomatoes and a bunch of
whiskered carrots.

The cottage seemed to thrum under the onslaught of the
wind. Doors rattled, a straggle of rambler rose branches
clawed and tapped at the window, and thin spears of
draught whistled through the air from unexpected quarters.

'No, don't move anything!' commanded Miss Vine
sharply when Alice eventually reappeared, tray in hand, and
hesitated by the cluttered table under the sitting-room window. 'Just put it on top of the papers – there's a fairly level

space beside my typewriter.' Gingerly, Alice positioned the
tray beside the old Good Companion.

'I've been busy getting this quarter's mag into some
sort of order – you remembered to get the new typewriter
ribbon?'

Alice nodded, placing the boiled egg, a plate of bread and
butter and a cup of tea on the small pedestal table that stood
by Miss Vine's chair.

'The girls' letters all have to be typed, y'know.
Everything has to be neatly prepared and then, once I've
composed my editorial, Barbara takes it all away and has it
photocopied.'

Miss Vine was gazing in some distaste at the papers that
lay in drifts on the table. 'Oh those damned letters with
their self-absorbed accounts of births, deaths, marriages
and divorces, illness, careers, successes and disappoint-
ments – and all the littlenesses in between. Life, I
suppose; and most of it so tedious! All those voices insist-
ing upon being heard; there are times when the clamour
deafens me and I'm tempted to make a bonfire out of it
all.

'I am filled with dismay, anger too, at the lack of
achievement of so many of my girls. I once had such high
hopes for some of them, my golden girls who showed
such promise in their youth. Or so I thought. Now all that
I can do for them is to help them keep in touch with one
another so that they can exchange the banalities of their
mediocre undistinguished lives and derive what comfort as
they are able from the realisation that they've failed no
more abysmally than their friends. Like an old-fashioned
district nurse I feel that as I presided at the birth I can
hardly evade the responsibility of laying out the corpse at
the end of the day when all the bright expectations have
finally given up the ghost! On occasion, when I feel less

exasperated, I'm inclined to suspect that possibly the fault lies in myself for having harboured such unrealistic hopes in the first place and then I find myself admiring their ability to make the most of things, to be satisfied with the second-best and not to weep over opportunities lost or never presented.'

'But surely that ability is an achievement in its own right? After all, very few of us can be expected to be seen to make our mark in life.'

Miss Vine shrugged. 'You may be right, Alice.'

She was silent for a few seconds, apparently intent upon cutting her bread into fingers. 'I received some rather distressing news this morning,' she volunteered at last, as though offering an explanation for her splenetic outburst. 'D'you remember Penny Lauder, taught biology at Beech Park?'

'Of course I do – wasn't she at your garden party?'

'That's right.' Miss Vine dunked a finger of bread into her egg and Alice found herself watching with an awful fascination its slow and shaky passage to her mouth. 'Such a fine woman, dear Penny. One of the best. Retired to Harrogate. Well, her niece writes to tell me that Penny's taken to wandering about after dark in her nightdress, knocking on doors, scaring the life out of her neighbours. Gone doolally, poor dear. Her niece has arranged for her to be admitted to Beech Park Home. Wants me to mention in my news notes that Penny is back in "familiar surroundings". Stupid girl seems to think my heart should be lifted by that!' Miss Vine gave a scarcely perceptible shudder and stared bleakly into her egg. Abruptly she straightened her back and added, her voice fierce, a strident counterpoint to the keening of the wind in the chimney. 'Horses get a better deal – send for the vet and *bang* it's all over!' Miss Vine turned the empty shell of her egg upside down in its cup and now smashed its dome with her spoon. She glared at Alice, defying contradiction. Then unexpectedly, she grinned and her voice light, almost sweet, remarked, 'A lovely fresh egg that, Alice. Thelma's very good about delivering a regular supply of newly laids, always excellent.'

Alice, facing the prospect of a greatly delayed lunch, regretted the caution that had prevented her from cooking for herself any egg found in that disordered kitchen. Miss Vine, polishing off the last of her bread and butter, was already looking decidedly perkier and demanded another cup of tea and a couple of biscuits from the barrel which was just visible under the papers on the table.

'Nancy came to tea the other day.' Alice found Miss Vine's habit of swooping from one mood to another disconcerting, but felt she was now looking quite strong enough to listen to what she was determined she should hear.

'Ah. And what did Nancy have to say for herself?'

'As a matter of fact, she had an extraordinary story to tell.'

'Did she, indeed!'

'It seems that Aunt Sophie developed delusions of poverty, or it may have been that she understood that she had money but didn't want to touch it. Bills just went unpaid, Nancy was given scarcely enough money to buy the barest essentials.'

Miss Vine nodded. She was pushing the biscuit crumbs on her plate into a neat circle, not meeting Alice's eye. 'And did she confess to you what steps she took to solve the problem?'

'Yes,' Alice hesitated, confused by Miss Vine's lack of surprise. 'Do you mean . . . did you know all about it?'

Miss Vine nodded again, smiling a little.

'But if you knew what was going on, why didn't you write and tell me? And afterwards, since I moved into Fernhurst I mean, you haven't given me the slightest inkling!'

'Well, dear, for one thing it's all over and done with now and, for another, I wasn't sure that I had the right to tell you. After all, it really is Nancy's story. The decision as to whether or not to tell you what she'd been up to was really for her to make.'

'But if you knew at the time, how *could* you let it go on! We are talking about the same thing, I suppose?'

'Oh, I expect so. Nancy started selling things off.'

She's enjoying this, thought Alice, nettled by Miss Vine's evident amusement.

'How could you have known – Nancy certainly didn't confide in you. Was it Sophie, did she tell you about Nancy's "solution"?'

'Sophie did find out, did she? Now that I didn't know. Well, I suppose that it was almost inevitable that she would, when one comes to think about it. Nancy hasn't the wit for intrigue, far too simple-minded. I never could understand what Sophie saw in her. No, perhaps it is understandable . . . Nancy's gift for unquestioning devotion does have its appeal. That sort of devotion requires so little in return.' Miss Vine paused and added, reflectively, as though thinking aloud, 'Funnily enough, there was quite a bit of that in Sophie herself. But the trouble with that sort of blind devotion is that it can become very burdensome to its object. One is inclined to draw away . . . the need to make reparation comes later.'

Alice, impatient, interrupted. 'But if Sophie didn't tell you, then how did you find out?'

'Surely that's fairly obvious! Paul told me, of course. Had you forgotten that I know Paul? I was instrumental in him coming to Tern Bay in the first place, you know. His sister – such a fine girl – has always been one of the regular contributors to my little mag. I like to encourage correspondence from Old Girls who've settled abroad; their letters give a certain cosmopolitan touch, don't you know. Well, when Camilla wrote to me and told me that her brother was scouting around for premises for his antique business in this part of the country, I suggested to her that he could do worse than look at the shop here in Tern Bay as I'd heard that the owner was thinking about selling. So, naturally, when he did take up business here, one of the first things Paul did was to call and pay his respects.' Miss Vine settled the folds of the quilt around her legs a little more securely and drew herself up a little bit straighter as though reminding herself of her own importance in the scheme of things.

'Did you know that the prices he was paying Nancy for the things he bought were, to say the least of it, very odd?'

Miss Vine laughed. 'Fortunately Nancy didn't realise that, but then the stupid woman had no idea of the value of what she was selling so couldn't be expected to question the prices he was putting on it. It doesn't bear thinking about what would have happened if she had got into the hands of an unscrupulous shark!'

'The lamp, the Tiffany – did he tell you about that?'

'Of course he did! That was the first thing Nancy brought to him. When she came into the shop that morning Paul didn't know her from Adam but apparently she was so jumpy and nervous that it stuck out like a sore thumb that she was up to something not quite above-board. When he made her an offer for the lamp of . . . what was it?'

'One hundred and fifty pounds,' Alice said, enunciating very clearly.

'Yes, that was it. Well, when he offered that and she accepted without argument, then things seemed even fishier. After all, the majority of laymen (and Nancy was clearly that) would have assumed that that lamp was genuine and would have been very indignant at such an offer. For a minute even Paul had been taken in by that lamp, it was a fairly convincing reproduction – certainly your grandfather had thought it the real McCoy. My word, your grandfather did make some frightful bloomers, silly fellow; made some hilarious mistakes in his time – as you doubtless know. That lamp was one of his worst bishes; heaven knows what he paid for it. Your grandmother never let him forget it. Don't you remember the way she always referred to it as the "Tiffany" lamp with such emphasis? The joke wore a bit thin as far as your grandfather was concerned. Your grandmother had a very spiteful streak in her, but I suppose one can't blame her for being irritated by some of his foolishness. He did have a good eye for a pleasing object, but he had no real expertise. Quite a number of his things are perfectly genuine, of course, but by no means all. Take his jade collection, for instance, quite a lot of soapstone there! Extraordinary how a man with such a talent for making money in the financial investment world could be so gullible when it came to his collecting hobby. He was one of those unfortunate people who couldn't tell the fake from the genuine – or vice versa. A failure of instinct, perhaps; a defect of temperament.'

Miss Vine paused and made a minor adjustment to the cuff of her grey flannel blouse. Conscious that she was rarely listened to with such rapt attention, she had every intention of taking full advantage of such a pleasing circumstance.

'Do you know, dear, I think I fancy a little something stronger than tea. Talking can be so exhausting! There's a bottle of whisky somewhere or other . . . yes, I remember. It's on the draining-board in the kitchen, I distinctly recall leaving it there yesterday after Paul and I had a little farewell toast. He just popped in very briefly, so full of his plans, so excited.'

Alice hurriedly fetched the bottle and found a glass only to be despatched to the kitchen again to bring a jug of water.

'You're still so quick on your feet!' said Miss Vine approvingly as she settled herself comfortably again, stiff whisky in hand. 'Now, where was I? Ah yes. Well Paul followed up Nancy's visit to his shop with a call at Fernhurst. He was intrigued, you see; he was sure her story was a tissue of lies. Then when he saw her at Fernhurst she told him another story altogether and that was so bizarre that he was inclined to believe that she was telling the truth and he got the impression that she really did believe that her actions were quite justified and logical. He guessed that in a small place like this, I would be bound to know Nancy's employer and Nancy herself, come to that. So instead of doing anything precipitate like rushing off to the police, he very sensibly came straight to me. In the meantime, on the assumption that she had told him the truth, he'd advised Nancy not to approach any other antiques dealer. Just imagine what might have happened if she'd picked on a man not as transparently honest and honourable as dear Paul!'

A flurry of soot pattered on to the hearth and Alice was instructed to sweep it up, which she did with such impatience that a haze of little specks continued to drift and settle in the draughty air for some little time.

'I suppose one really ought to fetch some newspapers and stuff them up the chimney,' Miss Vine mused. Alice sat mulishly unresponsive.

'Naturally I was appalled at what Paul had to tell me but I was sure that in normal circumstances it would be quite out of the question that Nancy would steal from Sophie. I told him to leave it with me for a day or two so that I could find out what was going on and then we could work out what would be the best course of action.

'The next day I called round at Fernhurst armed with a big box of books, magazines, fruit – that sort of thing. When Nancy opened the door she had to hold both hands out to take the box and that gave me the chance to barge past her and start climbing the stairs before she could prevent me.

'As it happened, Sophie was asleep but before Nancy had dumped the box and come haring after me – my dear, she was in a pet – I had the chance to take a really good look at her.' Miss Vine paused. 'Dear Sophie. She looked so frail, almost a stranger. And her room . . . well, the whole atmosphere told me that there was something radically wrong. Nancy shooed me downstairs but I headed for the kitchen instead of the front door and, short of violence, she couldn't very well turn me out.' Miss Vine gave a little laugh, her cheeks faintly flushed at the recall of her own cunning and triumph.

'My word, but she was cagey! Like a scrawny old hen defending her precious chick from a nasty fox. I could tell that there wasn't the faintest chance of her confiding in me; but she was clearly up to something. I can't tell you how cold the kitchen was – the whole house was icy. The central heating had broken down, she said. Well, I hadn't spent the greater part of my life coping with devious little girls without learning to detect a downright fib a mile off. Stupid woman, stubborn as a mule – it took me all my self-control not to give her a good shaking.'

'What did you do?'

'As soon as I returned home I sent for Paul. I told him that I believed that what Nancy had told him when he'd spoken to her at Fernhurst was the truth. Something had happened to poor Sophie's mind. She looked as though she hadn't got much longer to live. After we'd talked it all over, we came to an arrangement. Whenever Nancy needed money and wanted to sell something, Paul trotted along – all cloak and dagger, my dear. He'd pick out some of grandfather's more obvious mistakes for which he would then pay Nancy an exorbitant sum. I'm not surprised that you were puzzled if she told you what some of your grandfather's knick-knacks fetched!

'He'd pay her in cash and get her to sign a receipt which he'd bring to me (he insisted on that although, naturally, I trusted him implicitly) and then I'd reimburse him. All the bits and pieces he bought on my behalf are still there under the window-seat.' Miss Vine waved a hand in its direction. 'I've never known quite what to do with them. Now that you do know all about it, perhaps you'd like to off-load them on the vicar for the white elephant stall at one of his tiresome fêtes.'

Alice felt faint, black spots floated in front of her eyes. She remembered the drifting soot, dug her nails into her palms and pulled herself together.

'It was very satisfying,' Miss Vine was saying, her voice surprisingly soft, 'to have the chance to do something for Sophie. To make amends, if only in a small way, for having encouraged her – or, at least, not discouraged her – and then left her floundering. At the time, I didn't think . . . well, we all say that when it's too late, I suppose.

'I did realise that perhaps I should have written to you first, asked you to come down and sort things out. You had your own pressing preoccupations at that time. I imagined yourself and Mr Appleyard coming to a sensible arrangement:

Sophie's affairs taken in hand, Nancy pensioned off, Sophie ending up, at long last, tucked away in Beech Park. No good pretending that self-interest didn't influence me too. I felt that I had the right to take the opportunity to help her, to protect her from fuss and disruption for the little time that was left. I think that Paul understood that – although it was never discussed in so many words.'

'But what about Nancy! When Sophie found out what Nancy had been up to, she changed her will, cancelled her bequest.'

Surprisingly, Miss Vine laughed. 'I didn't know she did that. My word, the chap in the red jacket and blue breeches was really having a field day. Dear Sophie, she always could make awful errors of judgement – probably hereditary! I told you that her father couldn't distinguish the fake from the genuine or vice versa. But no, even in her confused state of mind I don't think that Sophie could really have believed Nancy capable of dishonesty. In her heart she wouldn't have questioned Nancy's loyalty! It's more likely that she resented the fact that Nancy was taking charge – poor Sophie had suffered having her life run for her for far too long. I expect she just rebelled. In a fit of pique she wanted to let Nancy see that she was still the boss and wasn't going to tolerate Nancy or anyone else "acting in her best interests" any longer. She'd have reinstated Nancy if she'd lived a little longer. One can't afford to act impulsively or out of pique when one grows old, there may not be time left for second thoughts.'

'I've put things right for Nancy,' said Alice, desperately clinging to the one spar that seemed to have survived the wreckage.

'Good for you – and just the sort of thing I would expect from one of my girls. So, there you are then – all's well that ends well, as they say.

'But there's just one thing Alice, a word of advice; if I were you I wouldn't let Paul know that you're aware of the whole story. I know it's only natural that you'd like to thank him for behaving as he did, but I'm sure it would embarrass him. We did talk it over together – as to whether or not I should volunteer the story and he was obviously relieved when I told him that I thought it best you should know nothing about it unless Nancy herself wanted to tell you about it. He was anxious that you shouldn't feel under any obligation to him; he so appreciates your friendship, you know, and didn't want it complicated in any way. I'm sure you'll miss his company while he is away; I certainly miss his little visits. I expect we'll both look forward to his return.'

'You think he will be coming back?' Alice's voice sounded strained, as though she had been screaming for some time on a mountain-top, unheard.

'Of course he'll be back, you'll see.' Miss Vine looked as though she was tempted to say something more but, checking herself, looked positively rogueish as she laid a finger to her lips and said, 'Such lovely surprises in store, Alice. Happy events to look forward to.'

Torn between a desire to get away, to be on her own, and a craven wish to postpone that confrontation with herself, Alice washed up the crockery in Miss Vine's stone sink and then, standing indecisively in front of Miss Vine, asked if there was anything else she could do to help. Miss Vine, looking rather self-satisfied, had rearranged herself in her quilted nest and said that she thought she would settle herself for forty winks.

'I'll look forward to you popping in again soon,' she said, making a fine adjustment to the cushion at her back. 'It's always such a comfort to have something to look forward to. It's a very good habit to cultivate, if one is able – pleasurable anticipation. For instance, while this wretched wind has its way, I try to keep my spirits up by looking forward to Saint Luke's summer.'

'Saint Luke's summer?'

'Yes, you know, that lovely mild spell one often gets around mid-October. I've known it last right into November! That's Saint Luke's summer. I've found primroses blooming again then, even the lilac fooled into sending out a flower or two. It's a sort of reprieve, the year's last fling, as it were, before winter descends upon us. It doesn't always come, but one can entertain the hope!'

Alice was scrabbling through the pigeon holes of the bureau, frantically searching for the scrap of paper on which Paul had written his address. April, startled by the flurry of papers that fluttered so unexpectedly to the floor, had bolted to the kitchen where she found comfort for her bruised sensibilities by filching the parcel of fish from the basket which her owner had so hastily abandoned on the kitchen table.

When the telephone started to ring, Alice was in two minds as to whether or not to answer it. In the act of tipping the contents of a drawer on to the floor (although reason told her she certainly wouldn't have put the paper *there*), the thought struck her that it might be Paul ringing her from France – Paul not yet in receipt of the letter posted only that morning. She sprinted to the hall, pleading aloud that the caller should not lose patience and hang up.

'I began to think I'd never get hold of you – I've been trying to get you for simply *ages*. I did begin to wonder if the gale had brought the line down, but then I don't suppose one would hear a ringing tone, would one?' Barbara, giving Alice no opportunity to reply, rushed on. 'My dear, have you heard?'

'Whatever it is, I don't suppose I have.'

'Goodness, Alice, you sound just like poor Eeyore! No, but do listen. I can tell you, I was absolutely thrown when Tom told us, and really it was just by chance that he found out. Mary told him a few days ago that she'd be going away for some weeks – well, she's always doing that, isn't she? She always leaves the key for Tom, you see, so that he can keep an eye on the house, turn off the water if there's a frost, that sort of thing. As it happened, he went round really early this morning to pick up the key from where she usually leaves it for him and that was how he saw them actually driving away together.'

'Who?'

'Mary and Paul Fellowes – off together in his car early this morning and looking as though they were over the moon. Well, that's how Tom described it, silly expression really, but one can guess what he means! She'd left a forwarding address on the hall table and it's somewhere or other in France. Mary, of all people – but when you come to think of it, one never did know just what she was up to. Talk about a dark horse – as far as I can make out, no one had an inkling . . . Alice, are you still there?'

'Yes. Yes, I'm still here. It's just that I thought I heard a door close . . . or perhaps one flew open.'

'Oh, this ghastly wind – it's always the same every year around this time. But, Alice, what do you make of it – isn't it the most extraordinary thing?'

'Yes.'

'I must say you don't sound all that surprised! I said to Jonathan that I wondered if you were in the know – you being a friend of Paul's. But you know what men are, they don't really put their mind to things, don't mull them over;

Jonathan just grunted and said nothing surprises him nowadays. Do you know, sometimes I think that I could dance a
fandango naked on the lawn and Jonathan wouldn't wonder
why, mightn't even notice unless the vibrations got his drat-
ted moles on the move. He's inveigled Tom into the mole
hunt now. I could scream! But *did* you know – about Paul
and Mary?'

'No, honestly.' Another ghastly realisation darted into
Alice's mind: on top of everything else, Paul had known the
truth all along about that bloody picture; he'd probably
even been with Mary when she was painting it.

'Well, I don't suppose you'd let on, not if you promised
not to tell.' Barbara paused but, Alice remaining silent, went
on, 'And Mr Burton – I bet you'll never guess where Mr
Burton is now?'

'No. But no doubt you're going to tell me.'

'Yes, of course I am! Actually, it's hardly a secret, the
whole of Tern Bay can see what's happened to Mr Burton.
My dear, he's in the window of the antique shop! He's
had some side-whiskers stuck on and he's been dressed up
in a sort of stuffy paterfamilias suit, high collar, gold
watch-chain, that sort of thing, and he's seated at a tea-
table that's all set out with Victorian china and silver. Oh,
and there's a little stuffed dog on a cushion near his feet.
It's all very eye-catching really, awfully life-like. I suppose
Mary doesn't need him any more, poor Mr Burton. I
thought his nose had a little chip on the offside, well, one
could say that it must have been put out of joint! Anyway,
a dab of plaster of Paris and he'll be good as new!'

'Lucky Mr Burton.'

Alice remained seated by the telephone table for some little
time after she had replaced the receiver. A herring head had
unaccountably materialised in the middle of the hall carpet,

but Alice's capacity for being surprised was, for the moment, quite exhausted.

She listened to the wind buffeting Fernhurst and resolutely willed herself to believe that when the autumnal storm had blown itself out there would be the summer of Saint Luke yet to come.

Warner Books now offers an exciting range of quality titles by both established and new authors. All of the books in this series are available from:

Little, Brown and Company (UK),
P.O. Box 11,
Falmouth,
Cornwall TR10 9EN.

Alternatively you may fax your order to the above address.
Fax No: 01326 317444
Telephone No: 01326 317200
E-mail: books@barni.avel.co.uk

Payments can be made as follows: cheque, postal order (payable to Little, Brown and Company) or by credit cards, Visa/Access. Do not send cash or currency. UK customers and B.F.P.O. please allow £1.00 for postage and packing for the first book, plus 50p for the second book, plus 30p for each additional book up to a maximum charge of £3.00 (7 books plus).

Overseas customers including Ireland, please allow £2.00 for the first book plus £1.00 for the second book, plus 50p for each additional book.

NAME (Block Letters) ....

....

ADDRESS ....

....

....

☐ I enclose my remittance for ....
☐ I wish to pay by Access/Visa Card

Number ☐☐☐☐☐☐☐☐☐☐☐☐☐☐☐☐

Card Expiry Date ☐☐☐☐